I0687624

JASPIERRE'S DESCENT

Mixi J Applebottom

Printed in the United States of America

First Printing, 2015

ISBN 978-0-692-59992-1

www.MixiJApplebottom.com

Life is crazy.

Thanks for reading.

CHAPTER

ONE

Jaspierre sat sullenly by her pool deck. She ran the sword down the sharpening block. A thin, determined sneer sat upon her lips. The metal squealed delightfully as it sharpened.

Chance was dead and gone. The blade let out a cry as the block rubbed tightly against it. Lucas was dead and gone. What was left for her? It had been three months. The edge squealed.

Mother would know what to do next. Mother would have created something new. A new experiment. A new love. Anything. Mother would never wallow. But Jaspierre was different; try as she had, she couldn't stay as cold and calculated as Mother always was. Mother never got caught up in guilt or love or misery. She just did whatever she wanted.

Jaspierre didn't want anything new. She wanted the old things. Her heart ached and screamed every moment she thought of the sweet, delicious man she had locked away. She had only been down there once since Lucas had been murdered. It was so heartbreaking. Her blade screamed as loud as her broken heart. It was so empty. His empty white cell, with his empty white bed. Her experiments with her cats were over. No more playing find-the-rabbit. The squeal of metal scraping metal grew faster and more furious. Lucas was gone. His head had been blown off his neck.

Chance had done it. Chance had taken him from her. She regretted setting him on fire in his house. She should have savored his death.

But it was too late now. Savoring was an impossibility. Ikali meowed tentatively. She ignored him. She had completely lost interest in her cats. The big, tall serval growled and lay down by her feet. He was hungry but willing to wait for her.

Jaspierre burst to her feet. "I should have diced up Chance. I should have saved Lucas. Why didn't I leave him in the car! Why!"

Tears flew as she swung the sword harder, chopping into the innocent wooden stool. Her swings were fierce and unwavering. Furious love and hate poured out of the blade and into the wood. Soon it was kindling.

She dropped the sword in the crumbled mess and stood, still panting. She didn't feel better. Nothing made her better anymore. She did need Chance. She needed vengeance. Again. A second time.

She didn't have Chance. *If I work it out with someone who looked like him...* Wouldn't Mother be happy?

She walked up the big, marble staircase into her room. Her short brown hair with a hint of silver on the sides was transformed by a long, dark red wig. She darkened her lips to a deep dirty red, and painted her eyes a dashing emerald color.

She dropped her long t-shirt dress into the laundry chute and stared at her closet. Hung in perfect color-coordinated rows were shirts and shoes and dresses. She ran her fingers along a few until she found the skirt she wanted. It was knee length, soft, and flowy. Who would even expect a blade to be under there? The dark swirling pattern was part of an expensive dress suit. She didn't bother picking up the matching jacket and instead slipped on a cream-colored shirt. Her breasts were almost too big for it and pressed tightly against the fabric.

She stared into the mirror. Her stomach seemed to be so round and lumpy. She frowned. Well, she was out to kill a dumb schmuck, so if it stuck out, it stuck out, she supposed. Her ass looked huge and round, and her boobies were so big, nobody would have time to notice how flabby she was.

Besides. They'd be too busy noticing the sword slicing up their skin. She laced up long, brown boots. They were fascinatingly tall and she didn't mind one bit.

She took a dark green purse with a sparkling gold chain. Nice to have a backup way to strangle someone if necessary. This would surely be a plan Mother would approve. She'd go out, move on, and find something else to think about. And once she had sliced up a poor Chance substitute, she would be back to her normal self and everything would be fine.

She clicked her heels down the steps and to the grand front doorway. Tessa sat in front of the door and glared at her.

Jasp almost shooed her away but rolled her eyes. "Fine." She clicked crisply away to the kitchen to open the four matching cans of cat food. She plated them and set them on the stand for the cats to eat. Ikali and Tessa hustled over and vigorously munched down.

Jaspierre hated the kitchen. Hated it. Everything she remembered here had to do with Lucas. The first time she met him, chased him, and locked him in the basement. The last time, when he retched at the sight of her maid's mouth gaping open from a blade. The times he cooked for her. That moment when he made her a salad. *Ha, as if she ate salads.*

Chance had killed him. The only person

who ever loved her. Fury rose within her. She needed to go unleash it so she could move on.

She clicked to the door in a hurry. The door swung open and slammed shut behind her. She walked to the garage and wondered which car to take. There were many makes and models to choose from, and she stared a moment before choosing her black Lexus. It was still one of her favorites. The one she had crashed into the lake had been sold, but this one, the one Lucas had driven, still called her name. It felt like they were a tiny bit closer, her sitting where he once sat. The door slipped into place and the engine purred like butter. Her sleek boot pressed into the pedal and away she flew.

The black sports car purred down the road like a hummingbird. She let the car go, skidding playfully around each slow, boring car with delightful pleasure. She knew where to go. She revved up the engine, letting the tires skid into place as she slid into the parking spot.

Today was her day. Today, she would find a way to get past all this. She walked confidently into the bar, and sat down on a large stool at the front, and ordered a drink. She turned casually and stared at the men in the room. Somebody who felt like Chance. Or looked like Chance. Or stunk like him. A surrogate.

She sat and waited. Nobody struck her as useful.

Idly, she twirled her straw into her drink and watched. There was a chunky bald man sitting in the corner. But he looked too much like a weakling.

She glanced at the bikers playing pool. Chance was not really a biker-type; he preferred big trucks to small motorcycles. She looked over at the young men sitting and laughing together. Screw that; they were practically babies.

Thomas, the bartender always had good advice, and she could ask him, but he probably didn't want to partake in a murder selection. She had purchased the bar a few years ago and paid him a little extra to be helpful whenever she needed. Usually, that meant swapping vodka for water when she was playing darts for cash. Never before had it meant choosing a man who didn't particularly need to live another day.

The chunky, bald man in the corner cursed at the waitress. Drunkenly, he slammed his fist into the table. *Well now, this is quite promising.*

"You bitch! You brought me light beer. Motherfucking light beer. Do you think I'm a goddamn teenage girl?" Baldy--that's what Jaspierre decided to call him--was quite the asshole. The room grew quiet as everyone turned to watch. The bouncy-breasted waitress stuttered and stepped back, but he reached out and grabbed her arm. "Get me the fucking real stuff."

Thomas, the tall, charming bartender,

looked much less charming as he picked up a bat and walked over to the table. "Do we have a problem here, sir?"

The waitress looked bewildered and frightened as she tried to pull her arm away before the scuffle started. His hand gripped her forearm tightly, though. Baldy stared at the bat and then turned and looked at the breasts in front of him, then turned back to the bat.

"Go ahead and hit her. I'm holding her still." His sloppy drunken grin stared up at the tall bartender holding the bat.

"Let her go." The bartender was cool and calm, tapping the bat in his hand. "Let her go."

"Why the hell would you get the bat, then! This girl needs to be taught a lesson. It was *light beer*!" His voice rang out across the bar.

"Let her go now." The tip of the bat pressed against Baldy's forehead and his grip let up. The waitress scrambled away. Baldy's eyes grew wide as he connected the dots. His hands went up.

"I wasn't gonna hurt her."

"Get out." The bartender stepped back and dramatically swung the bat, pointing it at the door. "Pay your bill and get out."

Baldy dropped a twenty on the table and stood up. He flipped off the bartender and stomped out. Jaspierre stuffed a hundred-dollar bill under her untasted drink and walked out after him. Baldy was cursing and kicked a trashcan.

His face was red and sweat trickled off his nose. She wondered how to approach him when he saw her.

"Oh look; the stupid pregnant chick came out to stare at the drunk old man. You want this?" He grabbed his crotch. "Fuck you. I won't be your damn baby daddy."

Jaspierre felt her face grow startlingly hot. As if he was one to talk with his fat, short body. "You want a ride?" She clicked the keys and her sparkling black Lexus flickered its lights and let out a soft beep.

"Is that your motherfucking...? Your car?" Dumbfounded, the man stumbled over and petted the black hood with his big meaty hands.

"Let's ride." She opened her door and got in, and they zoomed down the road. She drove fast and dangerous, skidding past cars and around turns. She glanced at Baldy, who appeared to be trying hard to keep his beer in his belly. She grinned and went faster. Soon, she saw it--that sparkling hint of a lake. She pulled up close to the beach. It was tempting to smash into the water like she did last time. It seemed hard to believe it was a mere three months earlier.

She parked and Baldy opened the door and vomited. "You drive like a man." Then he threw up again.

"Get out of the car if you're gonna be puking."

He obliged and stepped out. She got out and slid out her blade.

She desperately tried to take her time, but it seemed to be over so fast. She stood there, dripping with his blood on her body and her sword and found herself full of frustration. *Why isn't it working?* She halfheartedly hacked at his corpse a bit more. When would she be normal again? She should have taken him home and locked him up. Her stomach turned at the idea of this filthy, hideous man in Lucas's sweet prison cell. She rinsed herself off in the lake, leaving his body exposed for the wolves or whatever would find him palatable.

She changed into the outfit in her trunk: a soft white t-shirt dress with a dark black cropped wig. She slipped on flip-flops and dropped the blood-soaked skirt, shirt, and heels into a bag in the trunk. While she was behind the car, she clicked the license plate changer so every minute, one number or letter would change. Disappointment crept in. She had been feeling off for quite a while now.

How many men would Jaspierre have to kill to feel better?

* * * * * * * * * * * *

Edward sat at his desk, frowning. His brown hair fell into his eyes as he sat with his fingertips pressed together. It seemed they had a problem.

There were scores of bodies.

And a suspect.

This was, in Edward's opinion, the worst thing he had ever had to work on. He sat at his desk, ignoring the bustling police station around him. What if it hadn't gotten so out of hand? A house burned with multiple victims inside. What if he kept murdering so sneakily? Would he have ever been caught? Edward had to face facts. This was a serial killer.

A serial killer.

Chance Mickey Despoil, a cop who was or is a serial killer.

It was hard to tell how far down the rabbit hole it went. Who else had known? How long had they known? What had been covered up? At least a dozen hookers, by his last count. Edward never would have figured it out without that fire. Male victim sitting on the couch, head blown out. Female victim tied to a table, toes snipped off. Her arm had been broken. Everything else had burned. It was likely she had been raped, but who could tell? She was impossible to identify. Her dentures had melted in her mouth.

All of this taking place in a cop's house, in Chance's house. Chance was nowhere to be found. He had only been working at this police station for one year by the time his house burned down with two victims inside. It was unlikely anyone *here* had covered much up, yet. Chance's last employers had to have known, though. He worked there a full ten years. The body count must have been massive. He was averaging a murder or more every month, as far as Edward could tell.

Edward's boss did not appreciate transferring a murderous cop to his precinct. Edward wanted to nail that cop to the wall. More than that, it was his *duty* to nail that cop to the wall. But the Chief wanted this whole embarrassing affair to go away. A serial killer cop did nothing to promote the image the Chief wanted, and it certainly didn't make him look like he had a grip on his workforce. *Close this case, get it over with, sweep it under the rug.* His point of view was Chance was likely dead anyway, so no need to humiliate the force any more than necessary. *Close the case. Get it done.*

Edward was frustrated with the push to close the case quickly. Ed needed to find out what happened and how many women Chance had strangled and beaten to death. He wanted to do his job right, every detail; everybody accounted for. This wasn't a normal situation. This one was big time. Not just a cop who stole drug money, or traded a blowjob to a streetwalker instead of a ticket. This was a *serial killer*. He slaughtered. Diced. Mutilated. Tortured. He was smart. He used his position as an officer to hide evidence and point the blame in other directions. He wore his badge when he raped women and terrified them into silence. How could Edward rush this investigation? Too many layers. It would take time to peel them apart. Without a significantly larger investigation team, they would never know if Chance was the only serial killer. It blurred the lines of who he murdered and who someone else did.

When Chance's profile was on the news, hundreds of phone calls came in, but only two seemed pertinent. One was a streetwalker who explained she knew him. Chance had raped her and many of the other girls. He would pin them in a street alley, handcuff them, and toss them in his police car. She said nobody would ever admit it, but just about all the ladies had been attacked. She was glad to see him on the news. *Pin that rat.* That was what she had said.

The second phone call, Edward thought it might be Chance himself. A male voice said, "I saw him driving to Mexico." Almost certainly a lie, but interesting that Chance was watching the investigation.

The rest of the phone calls were complaints about Chance's behavior as a member of the force. This wasn't shocking, knowing Chance often used his badge as a tool to facilitate his behavior. However, Edward realized there were only two *filed* complaints against him. Two in the past year.

That seemed shockingly low for this man, if he was the man Ed believed him to be. He called the precinct where Chance had previously worked. They reluctantly faxed over all of Chance's formal complaints. He had eight. Eight in ten years. There had to be another paper trail.

Edward called back and asked if they had any documents on dismissed complaints. *Jackpot.*

They were extremely reluctant, and it took three phone calls and a written letter from the Chief for the files to be sent over. Ten boxes of dismissed complaints arrived a few days later in the mail. *Ten boxes.* It was obvious the files had been rifled through and large sections were missing. It didn't matter; these complaints were beyond the scope of normal police complaints. It wasn't just "too rough when arrested." Instead, it was "Forced himself in my anus, broke my fingers on both my hands." These were the types of complaints that had been *withdrawn.* Hundreds upon hundreds more sat in the boxes. What could be worse than raping and injuring detained civilians? Murder, probably. The murders must have been taken out. A full week of searching, and he found one extremely violent complaint resulting in death that hadn't been removed. "Niece had been detained for jaywalking; her left breast had been ripped from her body. She had been raped from every orifice over the course of several weeks. She did not survive. *Complaint withdrawn."*

It was time for justice. Chance had one hell of a head start, but Edward was gonna catch him.

CHAPTER

TWO

Jaspierre lay in her pool, staring at the plastered ceiling. She had been thinking about Mother a lot. Too much. Mother was gone when Jaspierre was a seven-year-old. Mother was twenty-eight years old when she left.

In a few short weeks, Jaspierre would be twenty-eight. She didn't have a child. She didn't have anything to show for her life at this point. The water sloshed softly against her skin while she floated. Not like Mother. Mother had experiments brewing and bubbling, and parties, and men, and her pharmaceutical company was flourishing. Jasp closed her eyes and felt the weight of the empty house. Who would she even invite if she had a party?

Twenty-eight. She didn't have a family anymore. Her father was gone – or dead. Hard to tell. Jasper was dead. Pierre was gone. One of them was her father. Not that Mother would agree. She said both were her father. Severina had held them captive for years, experimenting on them and trying to combine them into a perfect man. At least, Jaspierre thought that was the plan. Jaspierre closed her eyes and let herself sink into the pool. Hell, maybe it was just combining them because it interested her. That would have been enough for Mother. Most of the time, Jaspierre didn't mind being alone. It was preferable to the attentions of men and all that nonsense. But sometimes; sometimes, she simply wanted someone to love her. She had been loved once.

Lucas loved her. Hell if she knew why. She had locked him in those same cells in which Mother had locked her fathers. Jasp had always intended to kill him, but she just couldn't seem to do it. It was a shameful thing to be unable to take action. Instead of slaughtering, she simply waited. When she finally let him out, the most beautiful thing happened. He loved her. She loved him too, she supposed. Maybe that was why she never got around to killing him. Mother would have never understood that. Mother never knew love. She knew pain.

Jaspierre longed for a family. If Lucas had managed to keep his brains in his skull, no doubt they'd have started one. He'd have made an excellent father. She didn't have any grandparents. Well, none she had ever met. There was nobody to ask about such things. How could she have a family now? Stretched out in the water she almost floated under her waterfall, and kicked her feet quickly to avoid waterboarding her face.

Jaspierre's only remaining friends were her cats. Her big, beautiful cats. But, right now, she couldn't stand them. They seemed so needy and, on top of it all, they stunk terribly. They were painfully fragrant. Puberty maybe? They seemed too old for that. Maybe they were old. Old people smelled weird; perhaps that happened to cats too. She looked at the two cats sleeping on the cargo net. The waterfall poured from one side with their little jumping cliff. The other side of the pool crawled under the glass pane and into an outdoor swimming area. This was her only family. She had nobody else left. Not even a maid anymore.

Jaspierre wondered briefly what would happen to them if she got caught. She hadn't made much effort to hide Baldy. Of course, why would she even be a suspect?

Mother had always been so vibrant. So terrifying. She doubted Mother ever worried about getting caught. Jaspierre didn't often think about it either, but she was always wary. She had begun concealing who she was long before she herself even knew. Now she knew. She was a bad person. She was like Mother. That was why she had to hide. *Be aware, the world will snare.* She kicked her feet, pushing her body towards the side of the pool.

As she walked to the stairs, she noticed a spider web growing on the chandelier. She sighed. She would have to get a maid again soon. She climbed the stairs, her dripping wet body leaving a little trail up each step. She paused, looking into the workout room. It was way too big and unnecessary. She used to train some, learning to swish a sword with ease. It wasn't hard to win a fight. Almost everyone she picked a fight with was so unprepared a kid could have killed them. People were just big chickens. Scared of a little confrontation. Rarely had she even done hand-to-hand combat, especially not with someone who was skilled in combat. A drunken oaf was easy to dice up. Chance was another story. He could have killed her. What was the point of any training now? She didn't have any enemies left, any prisoners in the basement, or anything else. She had nothing and nobody.

She turned on the shower and lathered herself up, rinsing off and getting back out. She stared at her short brown hair with gray sideburns and was discouraged. All she saw was wrinkles and fat rolls and gray hair. She was such an embarrassment. Mother would be ashamed.

It seemed she couldn't stop thinking about Mother. Mother never seemed to struggle with guilt the way Jaspierre did. Mother was smart and terrifying. She'd just do whatever the hell she wanted, damn the consequences. If she wanted to see what was inside that dog, she'd just cut him open. Jaspierre couldn't seem to quite do it. She wasn't able to control her emotions like that. She seemed to be stunted by guilt. She was twenty-eight and murdering people still bothered her. Someday, she'd learn to shake it off like Mother did. Maybe it was just lack of experience. If only she had started out younger and been more consistent. Mother did say that she was dreadfully behind. A stupid, weak child. Was this all she would become?

She leaned to the cupboard to grab a towel and, somehow, she knocked the medkit out of the cabinet. The contents spilled all over the bathroom floor. Rubbing alcohol, wound spray, several boxes of antibiotics, tampons, and pads went sliding across the floor in a big clatter. She stared at the box of antibiotics and found herself sobbing. Those were for Lucas. Why did he have to die? She didn't want to be alone. Why? She punched the box and let herself cry until she had no more tears. Lucas was the only good thing she had ever had. The only good person she had ever met.

And now he was dead. The image of his face exploding next to hers played through her head. She opened her eyes, trying to avoid the memory; his proposal and her acceptance, his brains exploding on her face. *Fuck Chance*. He ruined her life. She shoved the contents back into the box and she paused as Baldy's words burned into her ears. "Oh look; the stupid pregnant chick..." Her hand hovered over a tampon. When the hell had she last used one?

Terror and excitement rushed through her. What if they were...? She whispered, "Lucas, we might be pregnant."

* * * * * * * * * * * *

After his house burned down, Chance decided it was time to lay low and recuperate a bit. He scratched his balls through his underwear. He found a whore who was more than willing to invite him into her house, and he had been staying there. It was a small, lousy, one-bedroom apartment. The kitchen was tiny, but the shower was wet.

"Inviting" might not have been the right term. She wasn't real excited to go back to her place, but he managed to convince her. It only took a few broken fingers until she relented. She wasn't real feisty; in fact, she turned out to be a real bummer in the bedroom. Not worth a dime, but price was right since he didn't pay a damn dime.

Chance had not made any attempt to go back to work. Surely the dead bodies in his house had been found; no way he could pin them on Jaspierre. The original plan might have worked if he had been able to dump the bodies at her house.

He stirred the can of tomato soup he was heating on the stove. He wasn't mad, though. Jaspierre always was a bright spot in his life. They had a beautiful give and take relationship. She was a keeper, that was for sure. He'd never felt such admiration for another human being. Most people were such worthless shit. He'd be happy to be in charge of reducing the surface population. In fact, in some ways, he considered it his American duty. Certainly plenty of women were only useful as a warm hole. Not Jaspierre; she was a real woman. Worth every bit of trouble. Who else would keep him on his toes? What other purpose was there for him? His nose wrinkled in annoyance. The only thing he didn't get was why did she say yes to that asshole's proposal when they had just gotten back together. Not that it mattered; pulling that trigger was so satisfying, brains on her pretty face. *Damn fine moment.*

He left the soup and went to the bathroom. As he pissed, he looked at himself in the mirror. He was naked except for dirty white socks and grey underwear. His flesh was still hot pink. The burn marks would become permanent scars. The skin was bubbled up on the left half of his face. On his cheek, a quarter-sized mark had burned deeper, to the third degree, the top half of the skin burned off completely. It was raw, bloody, pink, and gruesome. His left arm was about the same; blistered from his shoulder down to his pinky. A large chunk off the back of his arm was red and missing. It oozed. He probably needed a skin graft. His right thigh had been burned badly too. Most of the skin was blistered. Damn fire. A dollar-bill sized area near his butt was completely missing. He swore he could almost see the muscle moving underneath the raw. His veins stuck out and throbbed when he watched. He couldn't decide if he hated it or liked it. Yes, it did make him look more true to himself. But it also felt so revealing. Anyone could look at him and know what he was. The fear of the people around him pleased him, the few times he went out.

It was fantastic. And yet, he mused, it wasn't helpful to him. It made doing anything in public much more difficult. He'd have to soften it with a hat, sunglasses, a walker; things like that. For those sweet moments when he wanted to blend in. No harder than wearing his cop uniform.

He washed his hands and went back to his can of Campbell's. It had started to boil, so he grabbed a spoon and blew on it before he tasted it. *Eh, too hot.*

The room was filthy with trash and clothing and dirty dishes littered around it. The couch had one cushion cleared for sitting. The rest was littered. Chance had never seen much point in being tidy. He walked over to the bedroom and stared at the naked lady on the bed. Her eyes were wide open, like her legs. The pillow beneath her head was smeared brown from her recent hair dye. She vacantly stared at the ceiling, her jaw hanging. He wondered, briefly, if a corpse could give you head. Well, he did need to wait for his soup to cool. He went to find out.

* * * * * * * * * * * *

Edward read the case files again. Twelve dead women. They had things in common: most of them had brown hair or had their hair dyed brown. Some of them had their hair dyed brown post mortem. Chance was obsessed with brunettes. Many were of a similar shorter height, with larger breasts.

He had a type. Was he trying to replicate someone? His mother perhaps? It seemed like many crazy people were obsessed with their mothers.

He searched for Chance's birth records. His mother's name was Jennifer Despoil, his father was listed as Mickey Despoil. A quick search of both of their names found a news article. It turned out Mickey had shot her, shot Chance, and then shot himself. Chance survived, the bullet grazing his ribcage. If that bullet had landed where Mickey had intended, how many women would still be alive?

The picture was in black and white, Jennifer standing with Chance in front of her. He was four years old. Her hair was dark, and Edward incorrectly guessed that it was brown. Chance was then placed with his aunt – her name was Liddy Sakal; she was Jennifer's sister and barely nineteen when she took custody. Liddy married a man when she was twenty-three. Chance would have been seven. By the time he was ten, she went missing. Her husband, Jack, continued to raise Chance on his own until he turned fifteen. At that point, Jack turned him over to social services. He bounced around those last three years and then started working on the police force. His first job was in Scooner County, three states away.

Scooner was a large county with one medium-sized city, a lot of farmland, and a bit of mountain lands. He worked there from age nineteen to twenty-nine and then moved back here. Back to what? He had no family left here besides Jack. Would he want to visit a man that dumped him off in foster care as soon as the going got rough?

Edward thought about this a bit. The only reason Chance would want to visit would not be a good one. A few minutes of researching showed Jack still lived in the same mobile home park that he, Chance, and Liddy all lived in. Better pay him a visit.

An hour later, Edward drove up to the shoddy mobile home. It had probably been white at some point, but was coated in dirt and spider webs. He knocked loudly on the old yellow door. No answer. It was times like these that he was frustrated by the law. He couldn't just break in and see if Jack was lying dead in a pool of blood. He didn't have a warrant, and he couldn't get a warrant. A sick knot in his stomach turned.

"Hey! Whatcha doin' there?" a little lady yelled. She was sitting in a pink and white flowered dress that looked like a fat poncho. *Pajamas*, he guessed.

"I was looking for Jack. I had a few questions for him. Do you know where he might be?" Edward said.

"I reckon he's at work."

"Ah, yes." He should have considered that. He seemed to be getting a little caught up in his serial killer theories. "Do you know where he works?"

"I think he's painting houses, or he's helping with that baseball team. I don't know where he'd be," she said.

"Alright. Thanks."

"Is he in some sort of trouble? We don't see too many cops come 'round. We're more retirement park than anything," she said.

"No, not at all. I just had some questions about an old case."

"You mean his wife? Didja find her?" she said.

He hesitated. If he hinted that he found his wife, would Jack call back faster? Probably, but that was a pretty awful thing to do, and he was an honorable man. He tried to be vague. "I'm not allowed to discuss that, but I'm gonna leave him a card, and I'll give you one too. If you could call me when he's home, I'd appreciate it." He tucked one card into the doorjamb and handed another to the lady in the pink and white flowered sack dress that was probably pajamas.

He headed back to the office and got the idea that maybe Jennifer wasn't Chance's obsession; maybe it was Liddy. He pulled up both their driver's licenses. Both of them had red hair, not brown, but worse, they were tall. Nearly six feet each. Edward chewed his fingernail thoughtfully. *Who the hell was Chance so obsessed with?*

CHAPTER

THREE

Jaspierre stood in her bathroom. The floor was littered with pregnancy tests. She was sitting and waiting with a cup of urine in her hand and a test soaking. She watched as the urine ran up the stick and into the tester. She stared as the line appeared.

She was having his baby. Everything in life made sense again. She knew her cats weren't satisfying *because she was pregnant*. She understood killing Baldy didn't work *because she was pregnant*. Pregnancy hormones. It explained everything. She felt downright giddy. And for the first time in the last three months, things were going right.

But they weren't right. They were wrong. They were all wrong. A baby with no daddy. No daddy at all, and worse, no family.

Jaspierre paused. This baby was like her. She had no daddy. And of course Mother wasn't much of a mommy. Jasp would be an excellent mommy. She could cuddle. She'd never hit her child. It would be different.

But still. Jaspierre longed for her daddy. Pierre seemed like he would have done an excellent job. Why did he leave? Mother. Most certainly it was Mother.

But Mother had been gone a long time. It was time to find her father. Then they would be a family. Baby, Jasp, and her own dad. They could play ball, or whatever it was you did with your dad when he was growing old and you were an adult.

Jaspierre frowned when she realized what that meant. She would have to go through Mother's room. If she was gonna find Daddy, she would have to face Mother. Even *find* Mother. She stepped out of the bathroom and into her massive closet. She paused at the full-length mirror. She ran her hands down her soft blue t-shirt dress, holding her round stomach. How long until she could see it?

She found herself humming pleasantly as she stepped into the hallway. Ikali and Tessa both sat outside her bedroom door. Tessa continued to lick herself without looking up. Ikali let out a concerned meow. She reached down and gave him sweet caresses. It was the first time in weeks she had actually given him anything other than a plate of food or a door slammed on his nose.

He purred and she ran her hands all over

him. She kissed him. Jasp held him close and tickled under his chin until he purred at her. "We're having a baby. And I'm gonna go get my dad."

Ikali purred again. Tessa stopped licking herself and looked up suspiciously. When she saw the sweet, affectionate petting, she stood and stretched. She pressed her body between Jasp and Ikali, demanding attention. Jasp giggled and kissed her large feline. She caressed her kitties and told them she loved them. Jasp looked down the hall. She stared at the last door in the hallway. Soon she shooed the cats away and went to the door.

She hadn't been in there in years. She never wanted to go in there. But there could be clues. Clues! What was Pierre's last name? Where was he from? Where would he have gone?

She stared at the door. Then she turned back to her room and reappeared a moment later with her keys. She walked down the gorgeous hall and unlocked the door. The door creaked open.

Inside was a room three times larger than Jaspierre's. The bed was huge and dusty. Cobwebs covered the entire room. Jaspierre turned on the light and a cobweb sparked and lit on fire. It shriveled and fell to the ground, out as fast as it lit. The room was fairly sparse; a large bathroom stood to the right, makeup still sitting on the dusty counter. A huge mirror with an expensive, large white dresser. The dresser was hand-carved wood, painted and glossed. The mirror was decoratively carved, flowers and swirls – very elegant. The fine headboard matched the dresser – oversized and grand, each detail carved to perfection. There was a set of large double doors that led to her closet.

Jaspierre stared at the white dusty dresser. She couldn't imagine Mother would put anything important in her dresser. Sex toys and lingerie, probably a lot of nude pictures of herself.

She turned to the closet. The doors slid open effortlessly like the day they were installed. The closet was huge. Mother's dusty dresses hung from tired hangers. After hundreds of dresses was a handful of pantsuits and jeans, and then a longer stretch of lingerie and robes. There were a few shelves of dusty white scrubs. Jaspierre cringed when she saw them. Lucas somehow could haunt her even here. Behind the clothes used to be a door leading down to the little three-room prison that her mother had made. Jaspierre had changed it in the remodel, though, and that door no longer existed.

Jasp reached out and touched a red sexy dress and spiders fell from it. She recoiled and then pushed again, shoving the dress hard to the side. Behind the dress was a panel of levers, latches, and a metal ring. Nothing was labeled.

She flipped the first latch and a soft beeping noise started up. She turned and followed the sound. She found a small, dirty box on a shelf. She opened it and her eyes grew wide as she saw a beeping ankle monitor. The box had several of them. She leapt away and ran back to the latch to flip it off. She flipped it and took a deep dusty breath, which resulted in hacking and coughing. Just like Mother to have a bomb in a box activated by a switch. The beeping, though; there was probably a reason.

Pulling the ankle monitor out of the box, she examined the chain it was connected to. The whole thing was wired. When the switch was activated, the beeping started up again, slowly, then went faster with the countdown. Jaspierre clicked the chain into the loop on the wall and silence suddenly followed. She unclicked the chain from the ring on the wall and the beeping started back up. *Very interesting.* She clicked the switch again and silence fell.

She flipped the next switch, and another box beeped. She turned it off. The next switch was larger. She clicked it and a harness swung out from the closet. A sex swing. Jasp rolled her eyes and switched it back. Only two switches left. One she clicked and nothing happened. The ankle monitor was missing? She clicked it back in case she couldn't hear it.

Then she clicked the last one. Nothing

happened.

Damn.

She clicked it off and looked around the closet. There was a shelf with a few more boxes on it. She opened the first one and saw it held furry handcuffs. She closed it and slid it back on the shelf. A small pink box she opened contained tiny little white baby shoes and a hand-carved rattle shaped like a kitten. It startled her; she couldn't imagine Mother saving her baby things. She ran her fingertips over the kitten face. It was smooth except for a little mark on the ear. She stared carefully and saw two tiny little dashes. Were these her baby bite marks? It seemed so crazy. Mother kept this. Did Mother love her? She stared at this box, completely confused. This box would have to come to her room; she had something of her very own to pass to her baby. The next box had pictures.

She flipped through them. Mother was in most of them. She was obsessed with herself. Mother and her when she was small. Mother when she first had Jasp sit at a board meeting; Jaspierre was only five. Mother with man after man on her lap and underneath her. Mother naked. Jaspierre quickly flipped through the nude ones, wondering if it would ever end. A small ring fell out on the floor.

Jaspierre picked it up. It was so small. She had never seen her mother wear anything like this. It was such a tiny white stone.

Why wasn't it in the jewelry box? Jasp stood up and walked to the big box in the closet. She was careful to look but not touch. She never knew which were laced with poisons. It could be a lie Mother used to say, but who knew? The rings were massive. The earrings encrusted with huge diamonds and jewels. The necklaces were elaborate, detailed, and expensive. They were all the same pretentious style. Jasp looked at the tiny stone on the plain little ring. This could not be Mother's. Mother would never have bought this. She never would have worn it. She never would have appreciated it.

Jaspierre slipped the little ring on her finger and found it fit the middle one. Where had it come from? She flipped through the pictures again and, this time, she didn't skip the nudes. Many of them were men and Mother. Nothing special. But then she saw Mother between two men. One of the men was chained to a wall. She stared at the man's face. She remembered that face. The angry, twisted face as he wrapped his hands around her tiny seven-year-old throat.

Jasper. She swallowed back bile in her throat. She had spent so much time trying to forget him. Her other father, the bad one. She closed her eyes and counted to ten. When she opened them, he was still there. His angry face stared at Mother. She was bent over and sucking him. The other man had a chain wrapped around his waist trailing down to an ankle. His back was in the picture as he took her from behind. This one was probably Pierre. She wondered if he was as miserable as Jasper.

Staring at the back of a naked man was not helpful, although something was out of place. She stared again at Jasper, and it came to her. *He had all his own skin.*

* * * * * * * * * * * *

Edward stood at the lake. There was a body, half eaten by wildlife. It was a bald, middle-aged male.

The lake, though, stood out to him more than the body. Not long ago, Chance had been at this spot. He had shown up after a car crashed into the lake. The current running theory was that he took the woman, likely raped her. Broke her arm, snipped off her toes, and then left her to be burned alive in his cabin. A woman they couldn't yet identify, other than they knew she wasn't young.

There was another man at Chance's house who was tied up and shot in the head. Could the man have been from the car that crashed into the lake? A review of the 911 tape, which only included the voice of a female driver, never mentioned a passenger. Many of his toes had been removed and allowed to heal. How long had he been a hostage? The man could not be identified either. He had no dental records; in fact, no fillings. There were no leads.

When the crime scene was first arrived upon, it was assumed Chance himself had been tied up and shot. Quite frankly, the detective at the time was pleased Chance was no longer breathing. Edward didn't even think he tried to find out what happened on that case. There was no task force. In fact, after a cursory review, it was written in the notes it was a sexual encounter gone wrong, combined with a house fire. *Sweep it under the rug and move on.* This pissed off Edward so much. He didn't like a serial-killing cop any more than the next guy, but it was their duty to catch the man and send him to prison, not protect the image of the police.

After the dental records came through months later, it was obvious this man was not Chance.

Chance, that bastard; he was long gone by the time they figured it out. That was how this investigation was launched. Edward took over. Edward would find out what had happened. He was a good man and a determined man. There were two known victims, but there were enough corpses that an educated guess was that Chance had slaughtered many more. Those boxes upon boxes of complaints surely indicated Chance had few inhibitions. He had to find more than evidence at this point.

The lake was quiet, with the soft sloshing of water at the shore. This John Doe had been killed in this spot. At first glance, it seemed the wounds were caused by a sword. *Who attacks anyone with a sword anymore?* The body of the man in front of him had been stabbed repeatedly, then picked at by wildlife. He had no wallet. A third John Doe. Chance was a hell of a lot smarter than anyone gave him credit. The tide had washed away any obvious signs of tracks – tires or feet.

Edward went back to his desk. He had to wait for the autopsy report before he would know anything more about the man at the beach. He called the phone number he had for Jack, and it rang twice before it gave him the message that the line had been disconnected due to lack of payment.

That little old lady hadn't called to tell him Jack was home yet either. He tapped his fingertips on his desk and wondered if he should drive back to the mobile home park and see if there was anyone who would let him into that white building. Jack's house. Jack would be crumpled up in the shower where he had been shot. Surely Jack was dead at this point. Maybe he'd be sitting in a recliner. Would Chance shoot him or stab him? Seemed he liked to use either weapon.

As he contemplated what had happened to

Jack, Jessi, one of the other cops, called him over to her desk. "You are not gonna believe this. You know your man Jack? I think he just skipped town."

Edward nodded. *If Chance was after me, I'd run like hell too.* "Do we know where he went?"

"He's taken a kid, and he's on the run. He was coaching a little league baseball team. One of the mothers just came in to report that he was molesting her son. Now we've got a handful of upset mothers coming in, and he's got one of the boys and we can't find him. He's not home, he's not answering the phones; he's gone."

Shit. "Send me a picture of the kid. What's his name?"

"His name is Peter Mirabella. He's eight, curly, long blonde hair and blue-eyed," Jessi said.

"Alright, I'll see if I can connect the dots on this one." He went back to his desk and sat down. If Jack was a child molester, why did he dump Chance off at social services? Did he get too old? Did Jack really run off with this kid, or did Chance finally make his peace? *What a shitstorm.*

JASPIERRE'S DESCENT

Chapter

Four

Jaspierre carefully plated food for her cats. She poured herself a large glass of water and made a small sandwich. Her fingers lingered on the cold coke can still in the expensive, oversized fridge, but then stopped herself. No more coke. She was pregnant. Besides, water was important for a growing baby. At least, as far as she knew, water was important.

She probably needed folic acid or... something. She sighed. There was so much to learn.

She fiddled with the small gold ring holding the white stone while she sat at the counter munching her sandwich. There was one other place to look, of course. But that was much worse than her mother's room. Much, much worse. She knew she had to.

This baby needs a grandmother and a grandfather. She walked to her room and came back down in boots, leggings, and a light sweater. She walked outside and stared at her marble staircase and the bushes trimmed to look like cats.

The sweet evening air curled up her nose in a cold draft. The barn was the only place left to look. She turned and walked to the back of the house. The footpath made of bricks was overgrown. In places, the bricks were completely covered in plants. Jaspierre would have to call the gardener and complain. The path bent to the left and after a handful of tired stairs, she made it to the barn.

She opened the door. The barn smelled of fresh bright hay. It was tidy in here, the concrete floors recently swept by the gardener. An assortment of cages were lined up in rows. Large cages, small cages and a few small stalls. Most of the cages were empty. She walked to the room in the back and there were rabbits, ferrets, mice and a handful of other critters. They looked well fed and generally happy. One mouse was in quarantine, so it must have had a cold. The gardener was not neglecting the animals, at least. These pets were here for the servals, for her experiments. She hadn't put the cats in the maze since Lucas's last week down in his cell. Find the rabbit; that was always the game. It seemed pointless now. Years of playing with her servals, testing their skills, and feeding them live animals all seemed pointless. Jaspierre stared at them a while, watching the scurrying bodies tumble and crawl and play.

She steeled herself to go to the locked room in the far back of the barn. Not even once had she been in here since Mother disappeared. She took her time unlocking the door. Closing her eyes a moment, she took a deep breath, and then swung the door open. The lights turned on like magic.

The operating table was lit up brightly despite the dust. Bags of fluid still hung from poles around the table. Upon walking closer, she saw the dead body shriveled and wasted away. It was mostly a skeleton. A shriveled, dried body of dog perhaps. The limbs were not its own, though, so a rabbit or a cat too. Jaspierre had a pang of regret. If she had come in here all those years ago, she could have let it go. Like her dad, Pierre. *Run free, little furry friend.* But she hadn't let it go, she hadn't checked for it. Did it starve and wither like an un-watered plant?

She shook it off and tried to stay focused. She opened every drawer and cupboard. Mostly, it was medical supplies. An assortment of clamps and needles and razors and knives. There had to be notes or a desk somewhere. The thought of sorting through Mother's notes felt nauseating. What would she say? Probably horrible things, but hopefully, something useful. She didn't find anything other than medical supplies. She turned, ready to leave, full of despair, when she noticed the mirror. She looked closer at it and realized it was a one-way mirror; it was an observation glass. There were no doors on that wall, though. Where was the observation room?

She stepped out of the operating theater and looked around. The wall containing the door to the operating theater was a smooth wooden wall. Nothing stood out as a door. She walked to the corner next to the operating theater. It had to be close. This was the side the mirror was on. She knocked on the wall and nothing sounded particularly interesting. As she rapped at the wall, she noticed movement. She thumped harder and a little camouflaged latch swung out from the wall slightly and then fell back into place.

Bingo.

She pulled the latch. The door opened smoothly and she stepped into Mother's office. The lights came to life, humming and flickering on. The desk was littered with all sorts of pieces of paper. There were several file cabinets lined on the wall in the most orderly of ways. But Jaspierre couldn't look. She couldn't find a way to tear her eyes away from Mother's chair. Her chair had someone in it.

Mother sat in a long red dress, her sparkling gold heels peeking out from underneath it. Her long hair was hanging down. Her gloved arms were leaned forwards, and she stared at the desk.

Jaspierre garbled back a noise. Bile rose in her throat. Jasp stepped back and tripped, crashing to the ground. She cowered, waiting for Mother to turn and hit her. Mother didn't move.

Jasp stood. She stared at Mother. She tried to speak, but found she had no voice. She stepped closer and touched Mother's shoulder. Her skull fell off her body and rolled off the desk and hit the floor. Jasp stood back, trembling. Relief and sadness both at the same time. At least now she knew where Mother was. She stared at Severina's decrepit body and tears welled up. Tears for herself, for her baby, for her childhood, and for Mother.

* * * * * * * * * * * *

Chance realized the problem was that staying in one place was dangerous. Corpses rot. And this hooker wasn't getting any fresher. Also, her phone rang a lot. Only a matter of time until someone dropped in to check on her.

He had hidden here for a few months, and that was as good as it was gonna get, he figured. His whole body hurt when he arrived, the skin practically still smoldering. But now, he was healthy enough to travel. The thing was, deciding where to go next was an issue. He wasn't quite ready to date Jaspierre again. He needed a better plan. She was tougher than he thought, plus he was in no hurry. He wanted to be at his peak.

His skin hurt, though. He knew a little about burns. Second-degree burns (the crispy parts) had all mostly healed, only the much worse third-degree burns still needed attention. His healed skin was stiff, white, and leathery, and also sore and extremely itchy. The open third-degree wounds had hardly healed; his cheek, the top of his right thigh, and his left bicep were still bloody and raw. These burns were deep; as far as he could tell, they needed skin grafts. Not that he was going to get them. Carefully, he wrapped them with gauze, trying to keep them as clean as he could. Who knew how long it would take for them to heal?

He needed a hideout. A proper hideout.

He took the hooker's keys and drove her blue Ford truck out into the mountains. He stopped by each cabin. If someone was home, he left; if someone wasn't, he looked for a key under a mat. It wasn't long until he found the perfect place. A dusty old cabin, which hadn't been used in years. The key was under the mat.

He went inside and examined the place. Dust covered everything. The elk head above the fireplace would have been sneezing if it wasn't already dead. There were three rooms: a bathroom, the bedroom, and an open living room/kitchen. This was definitely perfect. Someone's old hunting lodge. The newest magazine in the rack was already five years old. A small bookshelf full of hunting novels was completely covered in dust. In the only closet, there was a huge stockpile of wine and whiskey and canned goods. Whoever used to use it probably had gotten old or busy. At the end of the bed sat a large trunk with a padlock.

Chance broke the latch apart and opened it. *Bingo*. There were two shotguns, a rifle, and a crossbow. A huge pile of bullets and about thirty arrows. This was definitely a great hideout. The only downside was it seemed like it wouldn't be quiet enough if Jasp was here making a racket. He looked around and, under a bearskin rug, he found a small wooden trap door. Inside was a cellar; it wasn't very big and it held some extra firewood. If he dug it out a bit, it'd be plenty big enough for even the most enthusiastic woman.

Chance settled in and started working up a plan. This would be a good place to bring Jasp if he fixed it up a little. They'd raise kids, start a family. He'd definitely top Lucas's shitty proposal: tied up together on the couch, he proposes, she says yes, his brains splatter. Although brains splattering could be an excellent addition to a proposal, as long as the bride and groom survived it. In fact, his ideal proposal would be while he was gunning down civilians, driving a tank, and she sucked his cock.

He looked around for an ax and chopped up wood. He'd need straps, nails, and a shovel.

Maybe even a pickaxe. She'd learn to love it here without much convincing.

* * * * * * * * * * * *

Pierre slowly carved a little kitten rattle. He'd been working on this one for about a week. His hands weren't much good anymore. He was missing the ring finger on his left hand. The tips of both pinkies had been amputated, and the tip of his right ring finger was missing. They were a constant reminder. Every aching attempt to carve the wood, and his hands would cry.

His hands, or what was left of them.

He was lucky, he supposed, lucky that Severina had gotten good at swapping fingers. Lucky that he was young enough for them to take. He'd be swallowing a handful of medications for most of his life, but his doctors said he was lucky that she had given them to him. Or he'd have lost much more. Much of his skin grafts took too. He had gone to a few surgeons, but they were reluctant to peel off Jasper's skin and graft on some of Pierre's. So he had two furry patches on his chest that he shaved every day. It bothered him so much that he never dated.

Severina had ruined that for him. He was such a young, beautiful, trusting boy, and she destroyed him. She was his only love, his only opportunities for sex, and his ongoing nightmare. He'd wake up with horny nightmares that he was back in that cell. Back with Jasper.

But most of the time, he just moved forward. Shake it off, step forward. He ran Pop's Toys, his grandfather's toyshop. He hand carved most of the toys, and when he couldn't seem to get them done in a timely manner, he hired a few kids to help out. Most of the toys were simple, but sometimes, he'd get caught up and make a masterpiece. A little wooden jack-in-the-box with tiny wooden gears sold for three hundred euros or more. Little rattles, like the one he was carving today, sold for five euros. Pop's Toys, located in Paris, France, might have seemed a bit like an odd name. Pop once said he thought that tourists would love an exotic name. Up until that moment they had called him grand-papa, but once the store existed he was Pops.

He didn't mind the work; in fact, it was a nice way to sit and reflect. He made plenty to pay his bills and a little to sock away for retirement. He loved watching the little children show up with their big, wide eyes.

As he finished carving the kitten's ear, he felt a hot wave of recognition. This one; this one looked exactly like the one he made little Jaspierre all those years before. He couldn't bear to call her that, Jaspierre, so he called her "Kitten." Sweet little Kitten.

He made her bottles, changed her diapers, and stayed up with her all night. He told her stories and tried to keep her happy. She was one of the few reasons he hadn't broken. He was still himself; a good man, a man of substance. Jasper hadn't fared as well; he'd gone crazy down there in that prison cell. Now the only things Jasper had alive were chunks of his skin and a few fingers.

He set down the little carving knife and massaged his aching hands. *Little Kitten, where are you now?* His biggest regret was leaving her behind. How could he have possibly taken her with him, though? Running for his life from Severina, the woman he had hoped to marry, the monster that tore him apart. Tears trickled down his cheeks as he thought about that little girl. That tiny baby.

He had tried to report all the crimes when he got back to Paris. Pops was still around and after he had been seen by many doctors, they talked with the police, with lawyers, with everyone. But it was too hard. It was too hard to prosecute her when she was in America, and he was here in Paris. Eventually, he gave up. He didn't want to fight her anyway; he never had wanted to fight her. Fighting her would give her even more opportunities to win.

It was one of the few things he clung to when he was down there. He was better than her. He was kind and good, and he didn't have to kill her. Murder was something Severina did without any reason at all, it seemed. Pierre was stronger than that. He watched for escape, and sometimes, he felt like it would never happen. But he waited and hoped that he could return, still proud of himself for being the better person.

After all that, he still ended up murdering Jasper. He could never forgive himself for that. It was Severina's fault for destroying the man so completely. He was consumed with hate. Pierre helplessly watched as he tried to kill that kitten.

Beautiful Jaspierre, strangled by the man she tried to set free. Jasper didn't want out. He wanted revenge.

Pierre ran his fingers through his hair and waited for the memory to pass. It was over now. He was here, making beautiful toys for happy, safe children. Severina was never going to see him again. He was safe. He hoped little Kitten was safe too; by now, she had grown into a woman, and surely had gotten free. Often, he'd sit at his desk and plan to Google them, Severina and Jaspierre. Likely they'd have made the news for something, good or bad. But he was never brave enough.

What if Kitten had been killed that very night? He tucked her in her bed, and then Severina slit her throat? He couldn't bear it. It was better not to know.

JASPIERRE'S DESCENT

CHAPTER

FIVE

Jaspierre picked up Mother's skull and set it in the wheelbarrow. Mother's head sat in her own lap as it was wheeled towards the house. The brick steps were a pain in the ass to go up, but there were only a few of them. The path after the first set of stairs wasn't difficult at all, and soon she was rounding the final bend.

Jasp made it to the front of the house. She stood between her two large serval bushes at the bottom of the marble staircase. The columns at the top of the stairs seemed far away. After considerable effort to get the wheelbarrow up the stairs, she finally pushed through the front door. Then through the kitchen into her office. The two carved servals on the fireplace were white as snow. She dumped her mother's body in the gigantic fireplace. Ikali and Tessa came by, sniffing and scouting it out with great interest. They were shooed away. Jasp piled wood around her mother's tiny, shriveled corpse.

Her stomach hurt. All this lifting didn't seem to be good for the baby. She dumped lighter fluid on the wood, opening the dampers so the worst of the smoke would head outside. She reached for the matches and held them in her hand.

"Mother, you were a terrible person. I loved you very much. I am sorry you died." With that short eulogy, Mother went up in flames. The fire roared and, after about two minutes, Jaspierre realized she needed more wood. It took a lot of wood and a lot of heat to burn a body. Jasp should have known by now.

She unceremoniously dumped log after log on the body, letting each armful catch before she tossed more on. The fireplace was massive, but she managed to fill it with fire. The heat was incredible. She stared at the flames for a moment and noted the stink was less potent on an aged corpse.

She lifted the wheelbarrow up and trudged it back. Probably because the skin is much more fragrant than the bones. And the meat. Meat and skin smelled when you cooked. Of course, upon further reflection, she couldn't remember any other times she had cooked bones, be they human or otherwise. With this thought, she suddenly hurled in the grass. This must have been how morning sickness worked. Things that never much bothered her before now sent vomit to her feet.

Once back at the barn, she continued her search of Mother's office. It was much less intimidating now. The desk and files were full to the brim with experiment after experiment. There was an entire file drawer on Jasper. Pierre had only two large file folders. Jaspierre wondered how much longer Jasper had been in captivity than Pierre.

The notes on Pierre were short and not terribly useful. *"Subject B keeps pleading to see the baby. I gave him a cat skeleton and he sobbed. What a fun prank. It only took him an hour to figure it out, though."* It was dated for two months after Jasp's birth. Five years later, the file got interesting. "Subject BA is handling transplants well. It looks like he might grow furrier than I was expecting."

Subject BA. This must have been when she swapped and combined them. Jasper's hairy skin was being stitched to Pierre. Even after reading the whole file, there was no more information on who Pierre was. Subject B and Subject BA didn't indicate where he would have gone, or where he was from.

Jasp closed his file and sat a moment. She could read Jasper's file next, but a book caught her eye. She dug in the desk and found two old diaries from Mother. This looked much more promising. She took both of them and a caffeine headache called her name. She closed up the barn and walked back to the house. She went up the stairs holding the books with one hand and her head with the other.

Mother burning still seemed so light compared to the dark stench of a full corpse. Nausea hit her, and she retched properly in a sink this time. Her head was now throbbing. It was hard to quit caffeine! For the sake of the baby, she would do it, though. She carried a few more logs to the fire and sat in her chair and watched for a bit. She needed to hire a new maid. Mother had a hiring website for those special people with the ability to be discreet: Viscardine. Jaspierre considered listing for a maid, maybe even a chef. A sparring partner might be nice. She didn't want her skills with a blade getting even worse. She sighed thoughtfully.

She shook her head, trying to shake off the ache. Her fingers pressed tight into her temples, begging for a bit of relief. Hiring people was so unpleasant. It seemed as the years went on, she wanted less and less people to be in her immediate life, meddling about. But now she was about to have a baby. Babies needed people. She'd need a nanny too, and all sorts of staff. She clutched her mother's worn leather diary in her hand. Two books. The aching pressure behind her eyes grew strong. Hopefully, one of these held the secrets of Pierre. Or at least would guide her on what to do next with her life. *What did Mother do when she found out she was pregnant with me?*

Screw it, she'd quit caffeine tomorrow. She popped open a coke and started reading.

* * * * * * * * * * * *

Look for the hookers. Edward stood staring at the body on the bed. She had been dead at least a month. Could be longer. She had been used for sexual pleasure long after she had been decaying.

She had been found because her body had stunk so badly the neighbors put in a call. This had to be Chance; it fit his typical victim pool (*hookers*) and his particular type (*large breasts, recently dyed brown hair*). Although he had the most obvious two clues that it was Chance, her toes had been cut off, her right arm was broken, and also her fingers.

Her phone was sitting on her nightstand. She had more missed calls than her phone could even count. Three numbers stood out.

Mother.

Candi.

Unknown.

These three numbers had the most missed calls listed on them. Edward dialed the first one. "Hello, ma'am, I am Detective Edward Darbonne. Are you," he paused to look at a bill sitting on the counter, "Lisa's mother?"

"What's she done now? I am not liable for

that child."

"Ma'am you might like to sit down; your daughter appears to have been murdered."

"No shit. She's dead. I figured," the woman spat out hatefully.

"Was someone out to get your daughter?"

"Probably. Not like I'd know. We talk on Tuesdays, but she missed the last eight. I was hoping she was avoiding me."

"Why didn't you call the police?"

"Why the hell would I? We aren't always on good terms. That dumb girl. I knew she would get murdered. I told her that she couldn't keep living like this or she would get herself killed. It's not a shock to me. One of her bastard clients, or her pimp, or her crack dealer, or whatever the fuck else. I knew this would happen. One of them would get her and kill her." Tight, angry tears started to fall. "*Fuck.* It's not like I want to be right. I've got to tell her father." *Click.*

Edward dialed the next number. Before he could say hello:

"Oh my goodness, girl! I have been trying to reach you for like months now! You are *not* gonna believe what happened! Where have you been? You still 'sick' or is it a pregnancy? It's been ages, girl!"

"Ma'am."

"That reminds me! I got to tell you that..."

"Ma'am."

"You ain't Lisa. Where is Lisa? How the fuck did you get her phone!"

"Ma'am, I am a police officer. We would like to talk to you about Lisa." *Click.*

Dammit.

Unknown number.

Probably her pimp. He dropped the phone into an evidence bag and took off his gloves. Hookers who got killed were hard to get information on. Their friends were all crooks; none of them wanted to talk to the cops. Their families were angry; they didn't want to talk to a cop. It made it almost impossible to get the information that he needed. He looked around at the room. The cabinets were nearly empty. All the canned stuff had been eaten or taken. Open, half-eaten cans of beans and soup littered the floor. Food wrappers were piled everywhere. She was nearly out of food. A sheet torn into long strips had been used as bandages. The used, bloody rags littered the floor too. Her medicine cabinet was littered all over the apartment, aspirin bottle on the couch, ibuprofen sitting on the bed, an empty bottle of Xanax sitting in the kitchen.

Chance had holed up here, at this chick's place; the timeline held up. His house was burned, he hid out for a week or two – who the hell knows where – but then he got this hooker to take him back to her place. Killed her, raped her, broke her fingers, snipped her toes, and waited for himself to heal. He dyed her hair. But it seemed like, with this many bandages scattered about, he was not healed enough to get back to regular business yet. If his skin looked anything like his badly charred house, he had a lot of healing to do. He probably realized she smelled too much and he'd have to move along. Where would he go? He didn't own any other properties around here. He probably had another hostage situation going on. The man was starting to crack. He didn't even bother wiping the place of fingerprints. He didn't give a shit if he got caught at this point. This did not bode well for when they caught up with him.

As Edward drove back to the office, he considered the idea that Chance had no desire to go to prison. He'd rather have a shootout. From everything that Edward had learned, Chance was going to be a problem. Men who didn't give a shit were the scariest, most unpredictable criminals to capture. Still, he had to find a way.

"Hey, Jessi?"

She looked up from her desk. "Yeah?" she said.

"Any luck on finding Jack and that kid, Peter? Any leads at all?"

"Well, we found his car at a pawn shop. But that's been it so far. It's not really looking very good. Mrs. Mirabella is beside herself. We aren't even sure where to look at this point. He's on the run with the kid or holed up somewhere."

He let out a sigh. "Dammit, I'm about the same. Bodies keep piling up, but I don't know where the hell Chance might be. If I could find him, it'd be easy to nail him; he left so much evidence at the last scene. Once the fingerprints and blood comes back, I can at least confirm it's him, but I'm already convinced. Have you tried talking to that old lady? She seemed to be pretty interested in Jack."

Her eyes perked up. "What old lady?"

"Well, when I went there, the neighbor lady talked with me about Jack. She thought he might be at work painting houses. I gave her my card."

"Let's go give her another chat," she said. They rode together in her cop car and stopped at the white house. There was a yellow police tape strewn across the front of the door now.

"When we searched the place, we found plenty of pedophile porn, but nothing to show where they might have gone. He had nudes of almost every kid on that baseball team," she said disgustedly.

"We'll catch him." Catching the horrible rapists, murderers, and child molesters was what kept Ed in this business.

They knocked on the old lady's door, and Edward regretted not getting her name. She opened the door a small crack and peered out at them. "What?"

She was in those same pink and white flowered sack pajamas. Edward said, "Well, have you seen Jack since the last time we talked?"

"No. Go away; I'm watching *Wheel of Fortune*," she snapped and started to shut the door.

"Ma'am, please, I just wanted to see if you know anything helpful. It appears he's taken a small boy. We just want to find him," he said.

Her eyes grew wide and she froze with her mouth gaping open. Suddenly, she slumped forward and fell on top of Edward. A knife was protruding from her back. A red stain was spreading quickly across those tent pajamas. Her blood flooded the pink and white flowers. "What the hell?" Edward shouted. Both cops froze, bewildered.

"They're running out the back!" Jessi shouted, turning to run. She pulled her gun, but they were too late. Jack was already climbing on a motorcycle with a little blond boy, squealing off before they could stop him.

* * * * * * * * * * *

Chance's arms were sore from all the digging. He had managed to make the small cubby cellar deep enough that he could finally stand up in it. It wasn't quite big enough yet, just a few steps in any direction, but he wanted to make sure his bride would be comfortable. He filled up three five-gallon buckets he found and then would dump them outside. It was slow going. He didn't have a ladder, so he made himself two steps out of dirt. He pissed on them and stomped them into shape every time he had to urinate. They were becoming pretty compacted, although the cellar was a little stinky. They weren't the easiest thing to climb up and down. Two steps wasn't really enough, but fuck if he was going to make ten. He slowly filled the last bucket and set it on the step. His arms ached at the effort.

Probably just another foot or two would be enough, then he'd need to build some sort of restraint. He'd been thinking he'd just tie her to the floor joists, hands held high above her head, mouth gagged. But how could she birth their children like that? He had to think it through a little bit more. Did women need to be lying down to have a baby? It seemed important. Of course, that'd be quite a few months away. First, he had to catch her, then he had to knock her up. Marriage the ol' fashioned way, caveman style.

He chuckled. This place did seem like a cave. He certainly did plan to pull her hair down here.

He stretched and his back creaked and ached. Once the buckets were pulled out of the cellar, he cracked open a beer. Guzzling it as quickly as he could, he cracked another. He took his time and showered, carefully washing the open wounds still on his face and leg. His arm was finally starting to close. He wished they would get better soon. He didn't like having to wait for his body to grow skin.

Better go kill himself a deer. Provisions would be light until he caught something big enough to feed him for a week or two. There was a nice meat-hanging locker outside in the shed. He imagined he could catch at least four deer and hang 'em. It'd be awful nice to stock up before guests started showing up. He went out and sat in a tree blind he found. He carried both the rifle and the crossbow. He'd never used a crossbow before, but he sure couldn't wait to try.

CHAPTER

SIX

It was strange to realize how little Jaspierre knew about her own mother. Her memories of her being beautiful and dangerous were terribly spot on. But it was fascinating. She, according to her notes, once killed a man for passing the salt too slowly. Severina rarely fired anyone, instead preferring for them to have wretched accidents. Many times, this meant that she had to pay severance to their families, but she still preferred it to firing.

Mother loved sex. As far as Jasp could tell, she had sex with anything and everything. Much of her diaries were details of her sexual experiments. Will this fit? (*It seemed almost everything did.*) How many women can she make orgasm in a night? (*Six*) How many men can she ride in a single day? (*Fourteen*) How many species could she give head to? (*Thirty-five*)

At some point, those experiments became

less prominent, and they soon focused on other things. Jasp wondered if something happened to quell her incessant libido, or if she grew bored with calling sex an experiment.

The rest was much more morbid. Her mother had become obsessed with portmanteaus. Combining words and things to make new things. She detailed her incessant attempts to combine animals. Rabbits and puppies. She called it a ruppie. Jaspierre had even helped to make a few of them. She remembered standing in the operating theater, handing her mother tools. Watching her snip, snip away at flesh.

"Ruppie attempt number 53. Day 1. This time, the legs appeared to have adhered quite well. Started using a vibratory table to increase blood-flow. Already started with antibiotics and saline to try to stall rejection. Day 2. I knifed it. Not scientific. But the back leg already died and the damn bitch bit me."

Jasp stared at the number. 53. Fifty-three. That was a lot of dismantled puppies and rabbits. She wasn't sure how to feel about it. None of them had even survived. Mother certainly didn't feel sorry for them, but Jaspierre felt a pang of guilt.

Mother wanted to take it further. Her list was simple. Ruppie, cameleopard, and sheeple. Three combinations. But she hadn't even succeeded with one. Well, actually, her attempts to combine Jasper and Pierre seemed to have gone moderately well. Was Jasper's insanity considered a side effect? What if Pierre had gone insane?

Jasp wondered if the reason Mother bought her a serval all those years ago was to use its babies in the cameleopard experiments.

She never succeeded at a ruppie, though. Jaspierre felt a pang of guilt she hadn't followed in Mother's footsteps and finished her work. She did seem like she was awfully close. If Jaspierre never finished it, all those dogs and rabbits died in vain. For nothing, for an unfinished experiment.

Jaspierre bit her fingernail, considering. She could complete Mother's work. What would it be like if Mother was proud of her? It would be a way to stay close. A little piece of family. What if this baby in her belly had her own pet ruppie? This beautiful baby would have a piece of Mother, a good piece, a happy cute pet, as a reminder of the grandmother that would never exist.

She shook off the feeling and tried to stay focused. Where was Pierre? She flipped through the pages.

Where were all the useful clues? This was hopeless. She slammed the book shut and walked to her room. She crawled into bed and her kitties leapt up with her. Angrily, she pouted, wondering what the hell she was going to do next. Tessa and Ikali both purred loudly, until their comfort drowned out her worries. But Mother and the possibility of a ruppie lingered in her mind.

* * * * * * * * * * * *

Pierre set the little kitten rattle in a drawer. He started to work on a small music box. This one had a little bear in a tutu pop up and a small windup key for the music. It played Pachelbel's Cannon. The tinny music rang and he glanced at the drawer. He started to adjust the latch so that it would turn on right as the box was opened, but found his mind wandering to that kitten rattle.

He shook his head and stared at the little peg that started the box. Ten minutes later, and it was perfectly adjusted. The little bear popped up, and the song started just as the lid was barely cracked. The bear in the tutu spun smoothly. It was beautiful. He glanced back over at the drawer. Finally, he reached in and held the wooden kitten. Its face was just the same as the one he had made her. He flipped his sign closed and sat back in his office.

He remembered sitting in his cell carefully carving that little rattle, holding Kitten while she cried. Feeding her bottles one at a time. Changing her little bottom. It was terrifying. That was what he remembered most. Severina sometimes didn't bring more bottles, and he'd hold that sobbing, scared, hungry baby. He sang her the only song he could remember.

A stupid song about bells.

Tears welled up in his eyes as he stared at the rattle in his hands. He had made so many of these, it seemed impossible that one would strike him so strongly. Something about this very one, the way the ears were carved so smoothly, and the way the eyes slanted just so. All it was missing was her tiny little teeth marks. He just left her there. He ran away from Severina, the most terrifying woman in the world, and he left his daughter. Why did he do that? She was just a little girl!

He covered his face with his hands while he cried. He was wrong. After all this time, Severina *had* still managed to turn him into a monster. He left Jaspierre because he thought it would keep *him* safer. Severina might not chase him, but she sure as hell would chase him if he took that child. It was the most selfish, horrible thing he had ever done in his life. Leaving that defenseless little girl behind. Letting her feel the wrath of Severina alone. Just a little girl. Just a kitten.

He could go look on the internet and see what had become of her. He should do it. She'd be a grown woman by now, if she hadn't been murdered. Or tortured. Or sliced and diced. Did she own her own fingers? Or had Severina taken them from her too? Little Jaspierre Kyller. What had become of her?

He turned his computer on, and then unplugged it. *No.* He needed to move on. Stop thinking about this little girl. Just stop. She wasn't a baby. It wasn't his fault. Severina was insane. Nothing she did was his fault. He didn't make her lock them up, or hurt them, or torture each other. *She was the monster.* He stared at his hands. His missing ring finger on his left hand. The finger that was supposed to hold a wedding band. She took his love and spit it out. How could he ever move on or marry? He couldn't even wear a ring. He had been dismantled and dissected. *Severina was the monster.* Even when he knew it to be true, guilt still haunted him. Guilt; he didn't struggle so much with the anger. It was the guilt that kept his nights sleepless and his love life empty. Guilt terrorized him. If only he could have loved Severina more, or convinced her or helped her. Instead, his words, his body, his attempts to help her to be a better person failed. And he left that little girl.

He threw the rattle back into the drawer and went home. Tonight, there would be no sleep, for his demons were restless.

* * * * * * * * * * * *

Chance briefly considered bringing a lady

home to the cabin. It would ease his boredom for sure. But he didn't need another corpse rotting away. He didn't have time for all that anyway; he had things to do. The cellar was completely dug out now and fitted with a little hole for an outhouse. He also had thought ahead to give her a little chair and some sturdy chains threaded through the floor joists.

He spent long hours doing push-ups and staring at himself in the mirror. He was completely enamored with his new burned skin. His face on the left side was sagging and white, with open blood-red sections. The skin was twisting into jagged lines as it healed. It was hard to smile on that side, and his eyelid struggled to do its job. It was beautiful. His face looked like *him*. It was more real and more intense than he had ever expected. He felt more alive than ever before. More human. He wanted more. If he thought he could survive it, he'd burn more of his face and skin. It was too fucking painful to do that, though.

All he could think about was Jasp. She clearly liked her men fit, put together, strong. Somebody she could look up to. Hell, he was all those things and more. His body had slimmed down considerably in the last few months. No diet had ever made him lose weight so fast. Burning most of his body had taken its toll.

Suddenly, it came to him; what he needed

was a tattoo. That would enhance this new look of his without the tedious healing required by more actual burns.

He had dumped the hooker's car deep in the woods. An old red truck sat at the back of the cabin; the keys were in the glovebox. He drove it to town and found a nice tattoo parlor. He was planning on tattooing her name across his chest and asking about enhancing his scars. *Make those suckers pop.* When he was young, he thought coating his body in tattoos would make him a badass, but he knew he couldn't do that if he wanted to be a cop. But now, he was already coated in scars, so why the fuck shouldn't he add pictures?

"Holy frick, man, what happened to you?" The receptionist stepped backwards and looked like she would run off like a scared deer.

"House fire," he said with a big grin. He was thinking about how her breasts were almost the same size as Jaspierre's. He was leering, but he didn't care. He pointed the rifle at her. In his other hand, he held a case of beer. "Call your tattoo guy."

She trembled. "Rick, get out here. Now. Rick." She stared at the rifle, frozen in fear.

A few minutes later, a man came out. He had tattoos covering every inch of his body, it seemed. "What the hell is going on here?" He spotted the gun and raised his hands.

"I need a tattoo."

"Come on back and let's talk about it." Rick nodded to the girl. She'd call the cops as soon as they left the room.

"Anyone else here?"

"Not today; just us," Rick said. He was calm and collected, like he wasn't afraid.

"Well, she's fucking coming along, then," Chance said. "I've got this girlfriend. I wanna tattoo her name across my chest."

"How long you two been together?"

"Like, fucking forever. Also, do you think you can do something about these burns?" Chance said.

"You want me to cover them? It's too early to tattoo them," Rick said, staring at the rifle pointed at him. His voice sounded nervous, even as he tried to play it cool.

"Cover them? Hell no."

The tattoo man looked over Chance's face. "You like 'em?"

"Hell yeah! Jasp gave me these as a reuniting present."

The man paused. "She burned you?"

"Sparks fly with this one!" Chance burst out into laughter. "Damn, we're freaky, but that's how I know we're made for each other."

"You know, I have this idea. If you like them, I could trace them with white ink and black ink, and then they'd pop. Not where it is still open, of course. I can't tattoo where it's open, and it's gonna hurt like hell. But I bet you'd look like a real bastard." His voice trembled, even though the words he said seemed friendly, and his eyes never left the gun.

Chance grinned so hard, his skin tore. "Hell yeah. Let's do it." The girl sat quietly in the corner while Rick worked on Chance. He held the gun on her the whole time Rick worked. "So, I figure, if you don't do a good job, I'll shoot her in the leg. And then the head if I have to. You got me? I won't be shooting you unless you make me. I'd hate to fuck up your art."

He worked in silence, the girl sniffling in the corner. Jaspierre was tattooed in his chest in a blood red. Rick was talented; he made it look like it was sliced into his skin. Chance was impressed; he couldn't have made it look more realistic unless he razored it into his chest.

Chance drank beer after beer and tried to ignore his constant boner while the man worked. Finally, he was ready to work on his face. Even as drunk as he was, the skin fucking hurt. His finger hovered on the trigger, trembling with the pain. "Hurry the fuck up." Rick tried to go as fast as possible.

"This would be way easier if you'd set that gun down."

"I bet it would be easier. It'd be a whole fucking lot easier to shoot her. I bet you'd get this shit done faster."

Rick hurried and worked on his face. The pain was incredible, much worse than the fire. The fire hadn't lasted as long. That fucking buzzing hurt like hell. Finally, Rick said he was done.

Chance looked in the mirror. It was perfection. He looked like a real fucking asshole. Someone who could control his woman. Someone everyone should watch the fuck out for.

He looked like himself.

He shot them both in the head and left them in the back room. He grabbed her keys and locked the door on the way out.

CHAPTER

SEVEN

Jaspierre idly sat at the head of the boardroom. She was having a hard time paying attention. All she could think about was her pregnancy and her father. She had no real leads. It was discouraging. Maybe it was time to hire a detective. Of course, then she'd have to explain to the detective that she was looking for a man her mother had held hostage, mutilated, took apart, and rebuilt. Ugh. That didn't seem like it would be a smart idea. Was anyone on Viscardine an investigator? Somehow, she doubted it. That place was more about keeping secrets than finding them.

The board was discussing the future of the company. What was the next big thing for pharmaceutical companies? She couldn't seem to find any reason to care. She had more money than she could spend in ten lifetimes. This baby could soon be the heir to this awesome job. She wouldn't make her start so early, not five, but maybe around ten or so. Maybe she'd even let her wait until thirteen before she had to head up any meetings. The board had a job to do, and that was to make lots of money, so she sat and listened to their boring ideas.

"The thing is, if they can print body parts, then they will need more anti-rejection medications because many more organs will soon be readily available." One of the men was talking.

"But that is stupid! If they are made out of their own DNA, then they won't need rejection meds. I think we should be backing out of them, not adding more!"

Jaspierre snapped to attention. "Did you say they can print body parts?" Her mind was whirling. Maybe she couldn't find her father, but maybe she could impress Mother. *Printing body parts.* What was the world coming to!

"There is this new technology. They can print a new leg with your own DNA or an organ or whatever you want. It's new, but it looks like it will be readily available in the next ten years."

"I want one," Jaspierre blurted out.

Surprised silence filled the room.

"Buying one of these machines is so costly, and what even would you do with it? We don't sell machinery; we only sell medicines. Besides that, it sounds stupid. It's the exact opposite of where we should be going! We don't want printed body parts. They won't help our bottom line," he told her.

"Oh really?" Jaspierre clicked a pen. "I believe it's time to let you go." He was escorted out of the building with a crappy severance package within ten minutes. She was so much kinder than Mother. Mother would have just had him fall from a ladder or get crushed underneath a forklift. Maybe she should have done it Mother's way. The staff here were all hired from Viscardine, a special type of people trained to look the other way. "Okay, so," she continued as though nothing had happened. "I want one. I want to play with it and see how it works. Send it to my house. This machine sounds like a game changer." She leaned in close; the board was intensely listening, terrified. "We are going to sell them." A roar of applause broke out. "Let's make it happen. This is the next big thing, and we are the next big thing. First person to sell twenty units gets a hundred-thousand-dollar bonus. We're adding medical equipment to our repertoire this year."

The meeting roared to a close, phone calls were made, and chattering excitement broke out. They sold two hundred fifty units before the end of the week. Jasp had hers delivered to the operating theater in the barn. It was bigger than she expected, about the size of a large refrigerator. A fancy computer sat next to it with a handful of other, smaller pieces of equipment. Mother would be proud of her. She was going to finally get her ruppie.

Maybe the hunt for Father was the wrong thing after all. Maybe what she really needed was something from Mother for her new baby. That was the kind of family she was used to anyway, just Mama and child, and dog/rabbit creation. Pierre was practically a ruppie anyway, with his skin and fingers swapped and changed. This was a better thing to focus on; finding Pierre was like searching for a needle in a haystack. It wasn't exactly likely to happen. Making a ruppie was just within reach. She better get started. Her fingertips lingered on the large machine as she examined its shape. She picked up the overly large instruction manual and started to read, glancing up occasionally, and wondering if printed limbs grew fur.

* * * * * * * * * * * *

Edward was looking through his files on the bodies in Chance's house. There wasn't enough of the man with no toes to do facial recognition. He had been blasted in the head. Even the woman, who still had a skull, didn't have many leads. The woman, though, she probably was the victim in the car.

The license plate the cop wrote down when he got to the scene led to people named

Hinkleberry. Follow-up phone calls revealed they didn't own a black Lexus, and they still had their plates on their current vehicles. So, somehow, the Lexus had their plate without stealing it. Perhaps it had been forged? The car itself had been towed from the lake, then was picked up by a male who paid cash. Edward couldn't get any further. The VIN number had not been recorded, possibly was scratched off, or neglected on the paperwork. After all, when they towed the car, nobody thought there was a crime scene. Chance had reported he was giving the driver a ride home, and the investigation ended.

The car crashed into the lake had been reported as a black Lexus. There were no missing persons' reports of an owner with a black Lexus. Three women had been reported missing around the time of the accident. One had been found dead already. Both of the other ladies were still missing, but only one of them wore dentures. This was likely the victim. Her husband was seventy-eight. He stopped in once a week to ask if they had found her. Edward still didn't know what to tell him. Just because he suspected that Helen was found in Chance's house didn't mean that he could prove it. Hell, he couldn't even get the DNA test without another, stronger piece of evidence pointing her direction. With no further evidence, it would be difficult to prove this was her.

She didn't drive a black Lexus; she drove a green Oldsmobile. They might have found her, but they couldn't explain any of the circumstances. They didn't know where her Oldsmobile was, or how she was involved with a black Lexus, or why it had the license plate of a couple named Hinkleberry. They didn't have any record of who picked up the Lexus at the impound lot, or who it belonged to. Her body had been tortured, toes snipped off, arm broken, and set on fire. He couldn't present Helen to her husband if he wasn't sure it was her.

Edward got a ping on his computer; her VIN number showed up. The green Oldsmobile had been sold by a man named Dan to an unwitting couple from a Craigslist ad. They had tried to register their car, and it was flagged as stolen. The couple didn't know anything. But they did have contact information for the guy that sold it to them. With teamwork, the couple called Dan and asked him if he could meet them and answer a couple of questions about the car. When he showed up, Edward cuffed him and took him back to interrogate.

"The woman who drove this green Olds is missing," he stated.

Dan's eyes grew wide and he muttered, "I ain't know about that."

"Either you killed her or you helped whoever did kill her. You better talk before I book you for her murder."

Dan sat silently.

"You'd end up with life in prison. You killed this sweet lady, and you'll go to prison for it."

"She ain't a sweet ol' lady. She had guns. I ain't got 'em no more."

"What the hell are you talking about?" Edward said.

"Look, I find this Olds sitting in the middle of my street, running, windows down. Ain't nobody around, so I think I'll take a look. On the passenger seat was two hand guns, and I pocket those, ya know? Can't let some kid find those. Ain't nobody coming around, so I think I'll drive it to a safer spot. So nobody takes it. So I park it at my house, and a few weeks go by, ain't nobody claimed it. So I sold it." Dan smirked. "Sold them guns too. Can't be lettin 'em lie around in the street like that. I ain't killed nobody."

"When. When did you find the car? Exactly when?"

Dan got quiet. "Does it matter?"

"It matters a hell of a lot."

Dan whipped out his cellphone and flipped through his texts. "Right here. See?"

He held up the phone; on the little screen was a picture of him and the car with the caption: *Got me new wheels!* The date was the exact same as the Lexus crashing into the lake.

It started to become clear. Lexus driver crashed into the lake, Chance is showing up any minute. Lexus driver takes Helen's car. Chance finds Helen at the lake and takes her to his house. Helen must have had a male passenger with her... with his toes missing? Too convenient. His toes had time to heal. The man was with Chance, not Helen. He could finally get a DNA test so he could prove to her husband that she had died.

Edward sat, contemplating Helen. She was in the wrong place at the right time. It was so unfortunate. She didn't deserve such a horrible end to her lovely life. Her husband would be so upset to find out what happened to her. Jessi waved her arm at him.

"Hey, you gotta come see this."

"Do you have a lead on Jack and Peter?"

"I do!" she said. He came over to her desk and sat down in the nearby chair.

"What's the scoop?"

"Well, after that lady got stabbed, I could only remember a partial plate on that motorcycle. But one finally came up stolen pretty similar to what I remembered," she said.

"Well, I was no help. I was a bit busy," he said, remembering the collapsed woman in his arms.

"Yeah, well, here's the thing: the motorcycle, they found signs of it in the woods at an abandoned cabin. This guy goes to his cabin for the weekend, and he finds the bike tracks out front, calls the cops. They search the place and it's obvious they've been hiding out. The whole place had been rifled through."

"Is Jack in custody?"

"That's the thing, we didn't actually find them. Maybe they moved on, but if they did, we have no idea where they went," she said.

"Are there any reported missing cars in that area?"

"No, but there are a lot of empty cabins this time of year. A lot of 'em."

"Are you thinking of taking a nice long drive to see if you can find something?" Edward said.

"Bingo. Wanna join me?" Jessi said.

"Hell yes."

JASPIERRE'S DESCENT

CHAPTER

EIGHT

Jaspierre stood at the pound listening to all the dogs barking. She had settled on it. A ruppie. Start where Mother would have started. In fact, it seemed like it would be an excellent beginning. She felt kind of giddy. She would have a family; ruppie and baby, Tessa and Ikali. If she could think like Mother, she could find Pierre wherever Mother had found Pierre. But it seemed a little too impossible. Without another lead, this baby would be grandfather-less. Ah well, at least she'd have her grandmother in spirit. She never would have gotten Severina's love, but maybe the ruppie would love the baby. Dogs were like that; they obsessed over people.

A ruppie wasn't Mother, but it was as close as she could get. A puppy, with rabbit ears and legs. It really did sound cute. Jaspierre had never done surgery on anything by herself before, but she imagined that it was easy to learn. After all,

Mother had no formal training either. Learn by cutting, slicing, dicing, and sewing. Her preparations involved purchasing a few vet textbooks and ordering some new stitching needles from the internet.

She felt kind of like a jerk. Chop the legs off a dog and print up a rabbit leg. Jaspierre wrinkled her nose. It was hard to like herself these days. But Mother would be proud. Wouldn't it be amazing to show this new baby Mother's greatest ideas? It could hop around the crib barking while the sweet baby played. Everything would be good again. Everything would be fantastic. This would definitely help her find her father. Thinking like Mother couldn't hurt a fly.

That was why she went to the pound. Here, dogs died if they weren't picked up. It should be grateful to be a ruppie instead of a corpse. She looked down the line of cages. "I want a young one, that heals fast." The staff person showing her animals paused. "I don't want it to die right away or anything," Jasp hurriedly said. She should have practiced in the mirror before she came. Sometimes, interacting with people was hard. They never really got her. The number of dogs astounded her. Certainly, it wouldn't be difficult to find a suitable one.

The person shrugged and walked a little farther. "Well, this one is young and hardy. It's missing a leg, though. Got caught in a lawn mower. It's nice and healed up."

Jaspierre grinned. Well now, this would be more like rehab than mad scientist stuff. She'd be improving a mangled dog. *Improving!* The dog would be grateful and happier hopping around. Dumb thing could barely walk anyway. It wagged its tail. This was a great sign; it was happy to see her. Happy to participate.

"I'll take it."

When she got it home, she found out it was a boy dog. She put it in the cage. It was missing its back left leg. She wondered if she needed to check on any muscles. But, perhaps she could print up any missing pieces. After shaving the dog, she spent the next few hours drawing on him with marker, finding and labeling muscles. A pang of guilt struck her. His big brown eyes looked so innocent. "Look, you would have been killed if I left you," she said, petting it softly. "You're a three-legged dog. Everyone would hate you. I'm gonna fix you up, then you'll have four hopping legs. You'll see. It'll be amazing."

It took her four days to figure it out, but finally, she set the machine to printing. This would be difficult, but it was worth the effort. Mother certainly would be impressed by this new equipment.

A week later, she realized she was in over her head. The dog was dead. She hadn't printed anything useful. The thing she had printed she thought was the right shape for a leg, but she must have put it in funny. It kept falling out and then the dog died suddenly. She couldn't figure out how to stitch those tiny tubes together. She had a newfound respect for Mother's skills. Time to get a doctor. Or a scientist.

She posted a job listing on Viscardine and had two interviews scheduled for the morning.

* * * * * * * * * * * *

Pierre had sold the kitten rattle at least three days earlier, but it still loitered on his mind. How could he convince himself to let it go? He couldn't be spending his hours with his shop closed sitting in miserable, terrible memories. Why did they haunt him so badly this year? He just couldn't; he needed to move on. The nightmares had returned. This would be the very last kitten rattle he would make. God forbid he ever have these terrible aftershocks again.

He pressed his fingertips into his temples. The bell rang and a tall woman walked in. She had dark brown hair and was in a tight dress with tall heels. She held the hand of a small girl around three or four. The little girl asked if he had any dolls.

He felt his hands tremble as he mutely pointed towards the shelf. On the shelf sat five little wooden dolls with perfectly curled locks.

Her mother looked so much like Severina that his heart was still pounding. What if this was what his baby had turned into? What if she had grown up to look exactly like her murderous, hateful mother?

It was time to sell this toyshop. He couldn't face the public anymore. He could hardly face himself. The little girl picked out a brown-haired little doll. He showed her how to wind the back with a key so it would take two steps and spin, then take two steps and spin. It was really a lovely piece.

The little girl shouted with glee when she saw the little doll twirl about. "She needs a song! I'll sing her a dancing song! *Oranges and Lemons.*" Just like he used to sing to Jaspierre. "*Say the bells of St. Clement's.*" The little doll twirled. "*You owe me five farthings, Say the bells of St. Martin's.*" Her tiny little voice carried clear and strong, but the music twisted in Pierre's gut. "*Here comes a candle to light you to bed,*" He turned away, trying to hide his sudden emotional surge. "*Here comes a chopper.*" The doll took two steps and spun again. "*To chop off your head.*" The oblivious little girl clapped her hands. "*Chip chop chip chop,*" The doll ran out of winding and fell to the table in a little dead heap. *"The last man's dead!"* She squealed and clapped her hands and took a little bow. "This is perfect! Can I have it, Momma? Can I?"

Pierre handed her the doll. "Just keep it."

He didn't think he could look at it again anyway.

"But, sir, this is a fifty-pound doll!" her mother exclaimed.

"Just keep it." He ushered them out quickly and shut the door. It was too much for him to watch a doppelganger of Severina and at the same time hear that song, that little song he sang to his little baby. Did Jaspierre look like Severina? He could have a grandchild. She could have had many children by now. What if they would accept him as family? He wouldn't have to be so alone. What if one of those children would want to work at this toyshop? What if he had someone to pass this beautiful legacy to?

He sat at his computer. *Google her and see where she is, see if she has children. See if her wedding was in the paper.* One quick search and he'd find out what Jaspierre Kyller, sole heir of Kyller and Co. was doing. His fingers lingered on the keyboard, but he couldn't seem to beg them to type. *What if Severina had killed little Jaspierre? What if all that waited behind that search was a short obituary?*

He shouldn't have left her behind.

How could he make this guilt stop? He couldn't face her; he couldn't even look. It could destroy what little spirit he had left. He couldn't keep doing this. He needed to stop; he was getting more and more obsessed. *Get over it already.* It was kill or be killed. Run or be held hostage forever. He should have run straight to the cops in America instead of coming home to Paris first. They couldn't do anything over here. He was safe, but Severina was still endlessly untouchably free.

If only he hadn't left that little girl alone.

* * * * * * * * * * * *

Jessi and Edward drove up a long, winding road. Pine trees settled in close to the two-lane road.

"This is a bit of a crazy case, isn't it? Jack, taking hostage a boy at the same time that you are hunting for Chance," Jessi said. She turned the car to the left, following the winding of the road. The trees were tightly packed together beside the road, making it difficult to see much.

"I can't tell if these two bozos are working together or if they are just both horrible, horrible people," Edward said.

"It is pretty awful. They say if you have a horrible childhood, you're more prone to this kind of stuff. So maybe it just all comes full circle."

"I dunno, but I sure am grateful neither of these people are my family," he said. "Hey, slow down a bit. It looks like this is where the cabins start."

She lifted her foot from the gas and the silver cop car slowed to a crawl. "I'd sure love to have one of these cabins."

"My father used to have one when I was a kid. Not as much fun as you'd expect: no electricity, no plumbing. It's basically like camping in a tent, with just a bit more protection from the storms," he said.

"Yeah, I suppose you're right. It would be kind of nice, though, to have a fireplace, and this fresh forest air," she said.

"Mosquito bites, gnat bites, and if you're lucky, there would be a snake in your boot, leeches in the water, and all sorts of mice and rats. No thank you. I'll keep to my civilized living." He gazed across the landscape, catching cabin after cabin. Most of them looked vacant. A few had thick streams of smoke curling out the chimney, but none of them looked suspicious. What he needed was one that looked like it was empty, but clearly wasn't. With any luck, Jack would be terrible at espionage.

"Do you see that one over there?" she said. She hit the brakes and the car froze in place while they stared. There were obvious motorcycle tracks, but no motorcycle in sight. A very thin wisp of smoke crawled out of the chimney and into the evening air. The blinds were all drawn in front of the house.

"Do you think these people own a motorcycle?" he said. "I guess I'll have to check." He typed into his laptop and searched the address. The owners of the house were the

McCoys, and they did not own a motorcycle. They owned a minivan and a small sports car, and neither tracks were evident in the mud. Suspicious, a little, but it could be that they loaned their cabin out to some person with a motorcycle.

"Well, think we should poke around a little?" she said.

"I think the problem with that is, that if we find him..." He paused. "I hate to have any kind of warrant issues, or to be let off on a technicality kind of deal. Do you have any good reason to knock?"

"Do you see that smoke there? Looks like that fire might be getting out of hand. I think we should probably knock and see if everyone is okay in there. Just a friendly house call; is your fire out of control?" she said, then winked.

Jessi hopped out of the cop car in full uniform and badge. She knocked on the front of the door. Edward wasn't terribly keen on this plan, preferring to play by the book, but it was already happening. He hopped out of his car, hoping there wasn't going to be an altercation, but it turned out that nobody was home.

The motorcycle tracks led to the back of the cabin, so without entering, they walked to the back. And there sat the motorcycle that they had been looking for. The same motorcycle that Jack wrestled Peter onto after stabbing a poor neighbor lady, and squealed away. It sat on its side and had a flat tire. This was the opposite of promising because it appeared that it had been ditched. What were they driving now? How would they ever figure it out?

"Do you think they're coming back here?" she said. "Because we could set up surveillance. Maybe the bike is down, but they're still using this place."

"I don't think it's real likely. If they were still going to use this place, they would've hidden the bike better. It seemed like a really bad idea to leave it lying here in the open," he said. "We should still have someone watch the place in case I'm wrong, but I don't think the odds are very good."

"You know, we could call the McCoys and see if they'll give us permission to go inside," she said. "If we don't think Jack and Peter are going to be back here, maybe we can find out something that they left inside that tells where they're going. That chimney was still smoking; they probably left pretty recently."

"But if they are coming back, then we would tip them off that we know where they are," he said. He considered her idea. Sometimes, in a case like this, you just had to use your gut. "Alright, let's give it a try." Ten minutes later, she had talked to Mrs. McCoy, who gave her the permission to search the cabin. Mrs. McCoy said there was no real reason not to allow them to search if they thought there was a kid missing. They'd be happy to help. In fact, the only thing that she particularly cared about was that they didn't break the front door. She told them there were two keys, one under the mat by the front door. And the other one was under a rock by the back door.

"Well, there is no key under the mat at the front door anymore. There still was a key under the rock by the back door. I'm guessing that's how Jack got in, by using the key under the mat," she said right before she unlocked the back door. They both went inside, guns drawn, just in case. The cabin was a little three-room cabin; bathroom, bedroom, and everything else. The fire had been burned down to a smolder, but it looked like it'd been fairly large at some point. They could've left hours ago.

A pile of boy-sized clothes sat in the corner. This was a soccer uniform; it even said "Mirabella" on the back. His long white socks with blue bands at the top sat under the pile. His soccer cleats sat by the fireplace. Either Peter was now running around naked or they had found him a new outfit. In the bathroom, there were chunks of blond curls recently snipped. Was Peter shaved bald now? Was this a standard haircut? It was impossible to tell these things from scraps of hair left over. The only thing they knew for sure was that Peter's hair was shorter.

Nothing else was moved. Even the canned foods in the cabinets were still dusty and untouched. After this quick initial scouting, they called the crime scene investigators to collect the hair, collect the clothes, and fingerprint the place. Even though this turned out to be a useful stop, it had not provided them with any new leads as to where Jack or Peter were right at this second. Jessi and Edward loaded back into her cop car and started the long drive back to the police station. If they had looked at just the right moment, they would've seen little Peter hiding behind a tree.

CHAPTER

NINE

Mother's site still worked just fine. Every so often, Mother had come up with an idea worth using. Viscardine was one of them. It was a job listing for *the right kind of people.* That was what Mother called them; *the right kind of people.* Everyone who had been hired in her company had been hired from this site. The first interview was at ten, and the second one at eleven.

The doorbell rang and Jaspierre was ready. She was in black heels, a green suit, and her long brown wig. She looked sexy, but professional.

When she opened the door, she saw a short fat man. He had an erection almost peeking out his pants. Clearly, he was excited to be here.

"Your house is so goddamn fantastic. Marble floors. Holy shit."

They walked to the library and Jaspierre couldn't seem to find anything to say in reply. She sat at her desk and motioned him to sit.

He didn't, and stood there with his crotch even closer to eye level.

"So, your name is Jeffrey?" she said, staring at her papers.

"Oh yes, that is my first name. It's a formality. I go by my middle name."

"And what is your middle name?"

The man was staring about her room completely giddy, barely paying attention. "Oh yes. Uh, Russell. I'm Russell."

"You have got to be fucking kidding me." Her heart was suddenly pounding and she felt rage building faster than she could manage it.

"No, no, not kidding." He turned to look at her. "How much is the pay again?"

Before he could get another word out, the sword sliced through his shirt and into his throat. She yanked it out of him and stabbed him again in the heart. She held him there, pinned like a cocktail wiener, and pushed him away from her desk, dropping him on the floor a few feet away.

What a total bust. The doorbell rang. She pulled the sword from the man, not even bothering to wipe it off. She dragged it behind her as she walked sulking. The sword rattled across the floor behind her, leaving a thin trail of blood.

She opened the door and lifted her sword. "You are early. What is your name?" It was a command, not a question.

He stood there, his eyes staring at the

blood-soaked blade.

"Your *full* name. All of it. Spit it fucking out or so help me." She stared into his green eyes.

"Dru Valentine Brummel."

She stared at him. He was tall. His hair was in a swirling mess. His eyes were a dark green color; he looked like he was in his early fifties.

"Do you need any help?" he asked, calmly looking at the blood dripping off the end of the blade.

"His name was Russell," she said to him.

He nodded. "Terrible name."

She broke out in a grin. "Welcome to your interview. Tell me about yourself."

They walked inside and Jaspierre took him through the kitchen, grabbing a few towels.

She wiped off the blade as he spoke.

"I have multiple degrees, I'm a specialty surgeon proficient in--"

She cut him off curtly. "It's your hobbies I am interested in."

"I like to take them apart and put them back together. I don't usually do it while they are alive. No reason to torture. That's not the point. It's so hard to learn without regular practice."

Jaspierre listened and put her sword back into the desk. "Put him in the fireplace."

Dru did, picking him up and tossing him in. "I'd rather we didn't burn him. He is still a valuable learning tool. I will burn him, if you want. But it's such a waste."

"Just put him in the fire."

He nodded and piled wood on the man's still warm body.

"Have you ever used a 3-D printer?"

"I have once. They aren't easy to get your hands on."

"I want you to finish my mother's work. She had an obsession, and I think you could do it with the resources I have. You'll have one month. You show me viable progress and I will let you continue. You'll stay here in the staff apartment. No other guests can come over. If you have a need for a hobby, you'll have to take it elsewhere. You wanna fuck, fuck in a hotel. No guests. None." She lit the match and the Russell went up with a *woof*. "Six figures. Three weeks off. Absolutely no communication to the world about what we are doing. This is for me. It is for Mother. But it is not for them."

"I'll mop the floors." And with that, Jaspierre had a mad scientist.

* * * * * * * * * * * *

After sorting through the evidence, it became clear that all of the hair found at the McCoy residence was Peter's. Peter had a shaggy long haircut last time he was seen, and by their recent estimate, he was either bald or had a buzz cut. They didn't know much else. Jessi went back to her own desk to work on her case, leaving a man patrolling the cabin. And Edward went back to his case, looking for Chance.

He found it particularly hard to focus on the serial killing cop when he knew that eight-year-old boy was stuck. He was stuck with the man who had created a serial killer. What if Peter was about to *become* another Chance? What if Jack was responsible for churning out serial killers, one after another? It was a nauseating thought. He just had to catch both of these monsters. He just had to. At least they thought the boy was still alive for now. It was good that he cut his hair and changed his clothes. He wanted to keep this kid. Probably for some horrible, terrible reason. But at least Peter was extremely likely to still be alive. *For now.*

He rolled around in his mind what he knew about Chance so far. Chance had mutilated and killed two people in his house. He killed numerous hookers in his old precinct. They thought he was going to make contact with Jack, either to kill him or team up with him. Nobody knew at this point if they had met up and were working together. There had to be some other reason why Chance came back to town. If only his aunt was still alive, she would almost certainly know what he was up to. How to find him, what kind of trouble he was in. Women always had an excellent intuition about that kind of thing. It was surprising how often a mother would rat out her child by sheer accident. By just talking, just knowing, just guessing.

Jessi walked up to his desk. "We think they're on foot," she said hurriedly. "We think they're walking around on foot! We don't think they got another car. Do you get what I'm saying? They're in the woods. They are wandering around in the woods right now!"

"What makes you so sure?" he said.

"We found footprints. No other tire tracks, and get this," she said. "We found more footprints this morning. *More footprints* than yesterday. They came back! Or at least Peter did. That's what we think."

"Holy cow. You think you'll find them?" he said.

"Yeah. We have a ton of volunteers; they are linking up and walking out. There's a good chance we will find him, today probably." She was all grins.

"That's excellent! I feel so relieved."

"It's really great. Hopefully, we really will find him." She winked. "I've got to go join the search. Good luck on your case."

This was excellent news. Maybe Jack had left Peter behind, and Peter was just wandering around looking for some help. He was probably too nervous to talk to any of the cops earlier. But when he heard an entire team of people calling his name looking for him, he would definitely come out! He was eight years old; he was a smart kid. Completely relieved, Edward focused renewed energy on his hunt for Chance.

The thing was, if Chance was still around, why hadn't he murdered someone else yet? Chance seemed like he was starting to spiral out of control. A thought stirred within Edward. *They must've missed a clue. Was Chance too injured? Did he leave town?*

Chapter

Ten

Jaspierre sat on the floor with Ikali's and Tessa's heads in her lap. Her round belly barely left room for both cats, but they were persistent. Her fingertips caressed both of their ears, and chins. "I hired a man named Dru, I'm not exactly sure if that was the right decision. He seems like a good fit, as far as scientists go." She lay down on the floor with her giant servals, and they snuggled up close as she continued to caress them.

"You see, I am sure he is the right kind of guy to make a ruppie. I can already tell he's got the knowledge. He is in many ways cold like Mother." The baby in her belly seemed to twitter at the purrs of the big cats. "I guess that's why I put you guys down here, even though I miss you dreadfully."

They lay together for quite a while before she finally stood and walked to the large console. She pressed a button and the glass doors slid open, but neither serval ran to their box. They were tired of the maze, despite it being as large as a football field and filled with mice, rabbits, and other prey. They preferred to be free. Ikali meowed desperately, walking up the stairs to the closed fireplace. Tessa hissed at the box.

"Come on, you guys. It's just not safe anymore." She pulled an angry Tessa by her jeweled collar and shoved her into the box. The big cat hissed, one of her claws catching Jaspierre's hand. The blood red scratch burned like fire. Jaspierre let out a yelp. Ikali came running over, but Jaspierre wasn't sure if he was about to defend her or Tessa. She shoved him hard into the box, her fury starting to build. He bit her arm, deep teeth marks sinking in. She shut the glass, and both servals were contained. Tears started to run down her cheeks as she released rabbits and spun the dials changing the platforms and walls to a new configuration. Tessa stayed in her box, meowing pitifully. Ikali ran forward and jumped on the rabbit.

Jaspierre cried hard. Her attempts to make Mother happy and to get ready for this baby were falling apart. Her only true friends, Ikali and Tessa, were growing angry and wild. How much more of this could she take? What else could she do? This baby was growing, and her family must grow too. She'd get Mother's ruppie, let her cats back out, and find her father if possible. Then this sweet little person growing inside her would know about all the most important people in her life. She'd learn about Mother and her obsession with portmanteaus and combinations. She'd learn about Mother's perseverance and coldness, and yet her ability to imagine. She would meet Pierre and learn about the strength of captivity and the beauty of being unable to crack under pressure. Her fingertips fondled the little gold ring with the white stone.

Like Lucas; Lucas knew how to handle himself. He knew how to take captivity well and use it to become the best version of himself. These were things that this new baby needed to know. They identified the past and would build the future. This baby would not be alone like Jaspierre was. It would have all the pieces of her family that Jaspierre could get.

Tessa let out a low, angry growl. If only the cost of these important things wouldn't be too high. Jaspierre put her hand against the glass door and stared at her beautiful serval. "This is for your safety, but soon the world will be right again."

She walked up the dungeon-like concrete stairs and slipped into the magnificent library. She closed the fireplace behind her, clicking on the serval's ear. She unlocked the library door and stepped into the kitchen to make a sandwich. Dru was already in the kitchen, and he said, "Where have you been?"

"I, well, I've been working in my office," she said a bit nervously. The biggest problem with very cold people like Mother was that they could be very dangerous. "Shall we go work on that ruppie?"

"Yes, that's what I was calling you for," he said. He opened his big mouth and crunched into a red crisp apple. They both walked to the barn along the dirt path. The door swung open beautifully. Dust swirled in the air as the sunshine flickered down on it. It seemed like she had just been in there yesterday, finding her mother. The fancy 3-D printers sat in the operation theater. "Have you printed something yet?" she said.

"Yes, I've printed a few things. I figured we'd start with something simple. See what we learn." He scrubbed his hands until they were pink and then slipped on medical gloves and a mask. Jaspierre joined him, but he was already picking up whatever it was that he had printed.

A young dog lay on the table. He was asleep, drugged in some way. She slipped on her mask and gloves and turned to the dog. It was a smooth brown dog. She didn't know the gender, not that it mattered to her.

Her imagination started to twirl. Wouldn't it be fantastic if they could modify this puppy into a ruppie, and then create a mate, then breed them? They would have the cutest little baby ruppie! It was impossible; it was not like they were changing the DNA of these animals. This was cosmetic surgery, not the actual creation of a new species. But, still, could you imagine the look on Mother's face to see a brand-new baby ruppie? God, that'd be amazing. Even cold, calculated Mother couldn't deny how fantastic that would be.

"Jaspierre, are you going to help or just stand there like an idiot?" Dru said. He clenched his fist tightly and took a slow breath "I... I didn't mean that. What I mean is, I printed the skin. So all we have to do is peel some off of the dog, and stitch the graft in. Would you like to start the incision?"

And hour later, she felt ashamed that he was so furious with her. She didn't do a damn thing right in his eyes, and his frustration was ballooning.

"Look, I need real assistants if we are ever going to get this done. I'll set up interviews and get them hired. You need to stay out of the lab and back in the kitchen where you belong," he bellowed with an angry tone.

Embarrassment outweighed her sparks of anger, and with her tail between her legs, she tromped back to the house. That night, she slept in her bed alone, missing her pets, crying over her inability to be a proper surgeon, and holding her hand with the gold ring on her belly, wondering if she would be a good mother, or if all her efforts were in vain.

The listing for new staff went online in the morning.

* * * * * * * * * * * *

Chance was starting to go stir crazy in the cabin. He never did like to sit around and heal. And frankly, it was incredibly boring without any kind of ladies to keep him company. He considered going and finding himself a companion, a thought he carried with him all the time. But this would be lousy timing to have a lady in his life. He didn't want Jasp to get too mad about him fooling around on her.

She consumed all his thoughts. Her bouncy booty, her round tummy, her big old tits. He felt like he was getting a little too old to not have impregnated her. It was time to start a family. He wanted the kid to throw football around with, to push a stroller, to smack around when he sassed back. He missed having a family. It had always been hard; he wasn't the kind of guy that did well with all that touchy-feely crap. But there were times that he missed his aunt, or even his mother. Mostly, he was getting tired of being alone all the time. Hookers were great, but they didn't exactly stick around. They weren't any fun out of the bedroom, so to speak.

Hell, they almost were not fun *in* the bedroom. They were always so picky. Don't hit me so hard – I don't like that – You don't pay me enough for this. *Blah blah blah, whine whine whine.* That was all hookers were good for. There came a time in every man's life when he needed to settle down and sow some seeds. He was a busy man, and his wild, partying college days had come to an end. Jaspierre was the only thing that mattered now.

He hopped in the old red truck he found behind the cabin and drove to town. He just couldn't sit around here any longer, so he needed to go get ready for his kids. He drove past a yard sale. It had a crib and a football. He took both and put them in his truck. The old lady running the garage sale didn't say a word to him. In fact, when he started to walk up to pay her, she waved him off, stepped inside, and locked the door. These new tattoos were awesome.

He was driving down the street, through another neighborhood, hoping for another excellent score, when he finally saw a pair of bikes parked neatly on the sidewalk. One bike was a man's bike with a child seat attached; the other bike was pink and still had training wheels. He tossed both in his truck and continued down the street.

He came across another garage sale. There was a nice baby swing, a couple of teddy bears, and brew-your-own-beer kit. He grabbed that stuff and loaded it up, not even asking the lady if she wanted any cash. *Screw that.* He drove off and she didn't say damn word to him. She probably didn't care or she found his current look terrifying enough not to care. Whichever. He drove back the winding road to the cabin.

He passed the cabin on the left; there were cops everywhere. He slowed down, watching the circus of people and cops. One of them held a giant sign that read: *Peter Mirabella, we love you, we will find you.* Curious, but he didn't stick around. It was still too obvious who he was. However, he was still wondering, who was Peter Mirabella? Why were they looking for him?

And much more importantly, were they going to search his cabin? What could he do to prevent them?

After thinking about it for an hour, and unloading his truck with all his wonderful supplies for his children, he finally decided that he was going to wait in Jaspierre's room until the search had slowed. He took his gun, his porn, and a fuck-ton of bullets, and he would sit there and wait. If they came in his cabin, they'd go out with a bang, party style.

Chapter

Eleven

Jaspierre posted two more listings on Viscardine. Dru suggested the position of assistant be two individuals, with specialties in cleaning and cooking. She almost protested. Two more people. Jaspierre was a private lady; she didn't want all these nosy individuals living in her house. But a cook and a maid were a sensible suggestion and, frankly, her peace and quiet was already ruined with Dru being here. So what was her beef with two more people?

He sat in the interviews with Jasp and soon they were four.

Basel Sane was a big black man, nearly seven feet tall and three hundred euros of muscle. He was primarily going to be the chef, although he had plenty of experience monitoring vitals. He had been a nurse up until he was caught. He had been drugging men in the hospital and forcing them to give him head. Or ass. He liked the power. Women were too easy to intimidate. He liked it when a big strong man couldn't even stop him. Nobody could stop him. After his nursing career abruptly ended with a stint in prison, he became chef at a large restaurant in town. He hadn't gotten caught drugging anyone there yet, but he knew his time was drawing close. Hence, the job search.

Dru loved him. He was, in his opinion, a perfect fit. He could do heavy lifting, he was trained in cooking, he seemed honest, and he had nursing training.

Jaspierre didn't particularly like him. But she allowed it anyway.

The maid they hired was named Arnold. He had white hair but said he was only thirty-five. He had OCD terribly and continually straightened objects in the room while they talked to him. His only bothersome hobby was breaking into people's homes and organizing them. He would organize them first by pints of blood, which he would bag and set in the fridge. And then he would remove each organ and lay them out by size. Hearts on the couch, livers on the beds, gallstones laid out on the toilet. He explained his system, but Jaspierre took little interest.

The four of them sat down for their first staff meeting, and Jaspierre started off with, "Don't shit where you eat. If you desire to have time working on a hobby, you better do it at least two hours away." She held up a tracking gun. "Trackers in each of your backs. Dru, if you would." He cleaned the gun with alcohol as she continued. "I don't like sharing this space. This is my home. I want our work done soon, then we will move on.

"Mother loved portmanteaus. Words like 'brunch,' breakfast mixed with lunch. Her life was cut unfortunately short, and I owe it to her to try to complete her works. She only had three creatures she wanted to make: ruppie, cameleopard, and a sheeple. She tried repeatedly and unsuccessfully to merge a rabbit and a dog. However, we have new tools that will make this much easier. Success is inevitable."

Dru pressed the trigger and the tiny tracker shot into Arnold's back. He grimaced, then continued to listen. Dru sterilized the gun again.

"Make no mistake, though. I have no hobbies. But I am a force to be reckoned with. If you mess this up, I will do much worse than kill you. Although I will do that too."

Dru pushed the tip of the gun into Basel's back and he grunted as the tracker pierced his skin. Dru sterilized the gun once more.

Jaspierre watched as Dru handed the gun to Basel, and he implanted the last tracker into Dru's back. "Let me show you your workspaces."

They walked out to the barn and Arnold

squirmed uncomfortably. Everything was out of order. The cages were in perfect lines, but they weren't categorized by size. His fingers start to twitch. Soon he was flicking them one at a time. *Four three two one. One two three four.* Fingers touched thumb, thumb to finger.

Basel opened and closed cabinets, familiarizing himself with the contents. Dru walked to the 3-D printer and watched the little squirting piston print. He was printing up another patch of skin to practice attaching.

Jaspierre stood and watched the men exploring the room. The half-skinned puppy lay dead on the operating table. Arnold entered the room and he let out a hideous whistle of air.

His fingers were thrumming faster, flicking, and his lips were moving as he counted. *One two three four, four three two one.* He grasped the ruppie and shoved it in the trash bin. He scrubbed down the bed methodically, then started on the floor.

Dru clicked his disapproval. "I wasn't finished with that one."

"It's dead. This place is so filthy, I can't believe you even tried to work," Arnold said mumbling, *One-two-three-four* as he frantically scrubbed.

"Dru, you can have Mother's office. I expect you'll keep her files and add your own. Any of her personal effects, you can file away."

She showed him the hidden room behind the one-way mirror. He grinned. He already loved this place.

Jaspierre left the three men to clean and prep and she went back to her house. It barely felt like hers now. She stood staring at the big marble staircase, the bushes carved like her giant servals. A hint of terror. This was the wrong thing to do.

She shook off the looming worry and went down to the library. She clicked the ear on the serval carving and the door swung opened. She shut the door behind her and was met by a loud yowl.

"It's not safe up there for you two." She stroked the big servals inside the glass boxes and kissed them both. She didn't bother bringing them any food. They would eat in the maze. And play in the maze. But they would not meet the new guests.

She shifted the maze around until it made a spiral shape. She pressed another button and a door opened in the middle. Ten mice came scrambling out. Two rabbits entered the maze from another button. A small fountain of fresh water bubbled up from the floor.

She pressed a switch and the cats were off running and playing. She found she didn't have the energy to watch them, though. This baby was already exhausting her. She fell asleep in her chair.

* * * * * * * * * * * *

Edward stood at Chance's burned up house again. He couldn't stop coming back here. An important clue was missing. He didn't know what it was, though. He had tried to call the morgue a few times, but they refused to return his call. He was gonna have to stop in later today.

Man on the couch, tied up, shot, toes cut off at an earlier date.

Helen on the table, tied up, toes cut off recently, arm broken.

What was he trying to do? Did he have a toe fetish? Did the other guy? So the guy on the couch, he cuts off his own toes. Then he decides to take Helen's toes, brings her over to Chance's house....

Except Chance found Helen near the lake. The woman was a random person. Were they a team? This man and Chance. But it went wrong. Chance double-crossed the guy.

Why toes? What did toes have to do with any of it? Who removed them? He lit up a cigarette and went for a walk. He walked down the road, puffing on his stick. A bird was clucking away on the side of the road. A big black raven, he thought. He wandered towards it, thinking about severed toes.

It flew off in a big whoosh, startling him. He looked over, and there were the half-eaten remains of the body of a man. A man with a severed head. Edward snapped a few pictures of it with his cellphone before he called it in. He wasn't shocked at all when they declared it was Chance and this case was closed. He would be moved to another assignment until the dental records came back.

That wasn't Chance and everyone knew it. This man had a broken arm and a severed head. Another John Doe. No pockets. What remained of his clothes appeared to be white scrubs. No shoes. *No toes.*

Edward didn't have a choice; he'd be off the case until the dental records came back. His boss wanted this case shut down. It was an embarrassment to their squad to have a cop involved in this shit. Well, at least he could help Jessi work on Peter's case.

JASPIERRE'S DESCENT

CHAPTER

TWELVE

Dru carried a bag of his stuff down the main hall, to Lucas's room next to Jaspierre's. Jaspierre stepped outside of her room, staring at the man. "What are you doing?" she said.

"Moving into a room," he said with a sly smile.

"You, Arnold, and Basel will all be staying in the staff apartment. Not in the guest hallway. You are employees," she said briskly.

"Hang on, now. I understand Arnold and Basel staying in the staff apartment. But I am the head scientist. I am the head person in charge. I'm the guy," he said angrily. "I should get to stay up here with you." He put his hand on Lucas's door. He twisted the handle slowly. He did not look up, his eyes boring into the door, his jaw clenched tightly.

"You are on the payroll." Her heart was pounding. She could feel the rage building inside her. What the fuck was this man thinking? Seriously? Why the hell would he think he could have Lucas's room! "If you want to stay on the payroll, then you need to get your ass to the fucking staff apartment."

He didn't look up. He appeared to be in his own battle of controlling his own temper. His face was twisted with angry, hateful spite. He opened his mouth to say something, then closed it again. He punched the door and turned to face her. "You need me way fucking more than I need you, bitch."

With that said, he grabbed his bag and shoved past her, her body slamming into the wall uncomfortably. Jaspierre was shaken. Who was this man? Who the hell had she let into her house? She stepped into her bedroom and locked the door.

What if that crash into the wall hurt the baby? Her stomach flipped, and she ran, vomiting profusely into the toilet. Should she have let him stay up in this corridor? Anger quickly faded into fear. He was just like Mother. Her mouth sucked dry at the thought. She couldn't control him, she couldn't stop him, and she needed him. It was just like Mother. She waited until it was dark, and then snuck down to her library, locking the door. Quickly, she clicked the serval's ear, and the fireplace slid open. Her bare feet slid down the concrete steps. At the touch of a button, the fireplace slid back into place, locking. For the first time ever, she crawled into one of the glass boxes, shutting the door behind her.

Her bare feet touched the smooth, cold, white maze material. And Ikali and Tessa were by her side instantly. She curled together with them, her head on top of Tessa's belly, and Ikali curled around her body. She grew warm and sleepy. She wept until exhaustion over took her. Why had she decided to let them into her house? Why did she have to make a ruppie?

* * * * * * * * * * * *

Dru sat at the old wooden desk and ran his fingers across the dusty top. He glanced through the one-way mirror at Arnold, who was frantically cleaning the operating theater. Basel was inspecting the rest of the supplies. He carried a clipboard he had found and was taking inventory. He made notes of things they would be needing in the future.

Dru stared at the two men, and then dusted his desk. While he was going through each door, he found a small latch at the back of one drawer. He tugged on it and a small compartment opened under the desk. Curious, he crawled under and ran his hands into the hole.

Inside was a small packet of letters and a passport. He flipped through the envelopes. They were addressed to Paris. He didn't bother opening any. A small picture fell out and he picked it up. A gorgeous naked brunette straddling a young muscular man. He was looking up towards the camera with a big grin. She was biting her lip and staring into the camera. The back of the picture said, "*Pierre and Severina made it to America.*"

The passport was Pierre's. The letters hadn't been mailed, although they were stamped. Pierre's name was in the upper left hand corner of each envelope. Dru realized he had found a secret. Pierre probably thought his letters had been mailed. *Decisions.*

Dru sorted through the files and the desk some more, but kept looking over at the letters. It was obvious this was Severina's desk. Her experiments. Her ruppie.

It seemed like Pierre probably would have wanted those letters mailed. Dru found a large brown envelope and slid the picture, the letters, and the passport inside. He wrote in the top left hand corner, "*With love, from Jaspierre,*" then he wrote the address in Paris from the old letters. He heard a rap on the door.

Basel stuck his head in. "So, boss, where do we order stuff from? I have the basic supplies planned, but if you need anything special, let me know." Basel paused as he saw the envelope. "Would you like me to mail that?"

Dru felt his heart flutter at the word "boss." Oh yes, absolutely mail this. He was in charge now. "Yes. I think there is a medical supply store about an hour from here. Be discreet about it, though. Do you still have a nursing uniform? Wear that when you shop."

"Yes, boss." Basel disappeared.

Dru programmed the printing machine. Once they had a puppy to work on, they would take tissue samples and put them in the machine. Then they could print up extra parts. Mostly, it had been tested on fleshy parts, like a heart valve. *No more waiting for the right person to text and drive. Smoke your lungs off and print up a new pair.*

Printing rabbit-shaped parts out of dog DNA had such interesting possibilities. He figured he would start with the ears. Dog-ear DNA printed to look like a rabbit ear. Legs, ears, and tail. That was all he had to successfully trade out to make a ruppie. He'd probably make two or three and then see if they would live. He grinned and got to work.

Arnold had scrubbed his fingertips raw, but the operating theater sparkled. He was done with the equipment and the floor and was humming and scrubbing down the cabinets. Even places that appeared clean to Dru were scrubbed multiple times by Arnold. After several hours, Basel showed back up.

Dru was still knee deep in programming. Arnold was clearly getting tired, but he relentlessly scrubbed. "I don't want to set these anywhere if you aren't ready for them," Basel said to Arnold. His grey hair was sticking to his face, and his fingertips bled on the counter as he scrubbed it.

"Onetwothreefour," Arnold blurted out in one big word and straightened. "Four three two one. Put them on the tray. I will get to them in a moment."

"I'm gonna make us lunch. I should have inventoried the kitchen before I left. You are tired, Arnold. You can finish tomorrow if you want."

"I cannot," Arnold said because it was true. He clicked his sore fingertips with his thumb, counting in his head.

"Well, I have gloves, at least."

"Good." Arnold slipped on two pairs and seemed less stressed.

Basel strolled to the kitchen. The little brick steps were old but perfectly usable. The yard was so well kept. He stared at the massive building in front of him. There was a grand circular drive up to marble steps. Two large bushes carved to look like cats stood stately on each side of the steps. The doors were massive and ornate.

He walked inside and looked for the chick. "Hello? I am making lunch. Do you want any?"

He walked up the marble stairs and looked around. The first room on the left was a massive gym. On the right was a locked door, presumably her bedroom. "Hey, lady?" He turned back and looked into the kitchen. Empty. He looked at the library where a corpse was almost finished burning. He threw a few more logs on the body and continued to walk around. "Hey, lady?" There was a massive pool; half of it went under a pane of glass to the outdoors. There was a big rock platform for jumping. He walked back to the kitchen and through the big dining room. A long, snaked table wove around the room. It was solid wood. There were little carved planks lined up across the table like train tracks.

He stepped into the kitchen. It was as elaborate and expensive as the rest of the house. He lit one of the burners on the six-burner stove with a turn of the knob. Soon, he was frying up chicken. He made mashed potatoes and green beans. Once it was done, he plated it all. The steamy hot scent of chicken tickled his nose. Getting it to the barn was definitely a problem. Carrying three plates wasn't terribly easy without multiple trips, and he didn't even have lids to keep the plates warm while he walked. He wished he had an intercom to buzz them and let them know food was ready.

He wrinkled his nose and set the plates in the warm oven, and he walked to go get them.

* * * * * * * * * * * *

Chance was sitting in the cellar basement again. There wasn't really anything left to do, but he liked to imagine her down here, in the cool, moist, dirty room. He kept envisioning her big, swollen belly full of babies. Birthing babies in dirt probably meant no clean up. Hose the pair off when they came upstairs, assuming, of course, that he'd let her upstairs some of the time. He wondered how many kids they would have. At least four boys. Enough to play a decent game of two on two basketball. The girls could do the cooking or whatever they needed to take care of the men. If Jasp was in a good mood, she could hang out up here in the main part of the cabin. He already made a sturdy chain to go around her waist. He considered breaking her feet so she wouldn't run off, but it seemed a little overkill. *Ah, this was love.*

Well, it was easy to get carried away once they started screaming. So tied up would have to do. If he felt like beating someone, he could always go find a street lady. They weren't worth anything anyway. With any luck, Jasp would be in a great mood and help chop her up. Jasp had a toe fetish and Chance wasn't gonna forget anytime soon.

The cabin already looked much different from when Chance first found it. Trash and porn littered every surface. Chance wasn't big on cleaning; that was women's work. The leash he made was a long chain, long enough to go outside and chop wood or fetch water from the nearby stream. Only after, of course, she had proved she wouldn't get to screaming and shouting. The dirt cellar had a strong wooden door he could slide a dresser on top of. If he left her down there too long, she could probably dig out. But let's face it; he'd be visiting her often to pump her full of baby seed. Nothing would escape his cop eyes.

He stockpiled canned goods; he wasn't planning on going to town much once she moved in with him. Damn, they were gonna have a fun honeymoon.

He hopped in the red truck and started it up. Time to visit the ol' fiancée. See what she was up to today. Binoculars sat next to him in the passenger seat. He pulled a hat down low and slipped on his sunglasses.

JASPIERRE'S DESCENT

CHAPTER

THIRTEEN

Jaspierre sat on the paper on the table. The doctor rubbed the wand on her round belly. "You look like you are pretty far along. Why did you wait so long to come in?" he said before looking up at the ultrasound picture. He stared quietly, and then said, "Well, I guess you aren't as far along as I thought. Due in early November."

Jaspierre wrinkled her nose in annoyance. She got it; she was fat.

He discussed the vitamins she should be taking and politely suggested she try not to eat too much. "Is the father in the picture?"

"He's dead. I'm a widow," Jaspierre replied curtly.

The doctor paused and looked into her eyes in the first moment of connected humanity he had all week. "I am truly sorry."

It was lost upon her, though, as she was already pretending to slice a blade into his belly for insulting hers. She still had some self-control, though, and held his bleeding flesh only in her mind.

She left the appointment and climbed into her car. Her long, brown curled hair was held into a soft ponytail. She didn't particularly want to go home. They were attempting to attach the ears to the first ruppie, and even though she was bound and determined to make Mother's dreams come true, she certainly didn't want to watch. Why did she feel so guilty? Was she the only girl in the world to feel guilty when trying to make her Mother happy? She should get over herself; everyone murders, tortures, and experiments. It was nothing to be ashamed of. Who did she think she was to feel bad for a dumb puppy? Her fingertips gripped the steering wheel so tightly they turned white. She didn't want to watch! Why was it so hard for her?

She had nowhere else to go, though. Dejected and discouraged, she started the car and home she went. As soon as she arrived, the scent of lasagna wafted through the air. Her stomach rumbled with anticipation. Big black Basel was plating in the kitchen. He pulled out another plate when he saw her. She smiled and thanked him politely.

"Do you know how it is going out there?"

"So far, so good. Attaching them is the easy part, though. Waiting to see if they are rejected is the game. We'll know in a week if they will stay adhered. He is already printing up another set."

He scooped up a square and placed it on her plate, and then added a small salad next to it, and a slice of garlic bread. It was as much a feast for the eyes as well as the mouth. And the smells! Oh, how they sang to her hungry body growing an entire person.

She resisted the carnal desire to eat. Basel made up the other three plates and set them on a white tray he had found. "I've gotta take this to the men." He carried it out of the kitchen. The moment he left, Jaspierre dumped her plate of food in the sink, running it down the disposal. She could never eat what Basel made. He had a reputation. And she; she had a baby to think about.

She made herself a sandwich and grabbed a coke and went down to pet her kitties.

Basel ate his lasagna and his garlic bread, watching Arnold scarf down his plate. As soon as the three men had eaten, Arnold suddenly drooped.

Dru glanced up at Basel. "What's all this about?"

"You've seen him. That man needs to chill out," Basel replied. Arnold's stringy gray hair was pulled into a ponytail.

"You better not screw me while I sleep." His dreary, sleepy voice barely squeaked out before he slept. Basel set his plate down and picked up the sleeping man, tossing him over his shoulder. "I'll go put him in his bed."

Dru grinned. "If you screw with him, you know that'll be the end of this for you."

"Mind your own business and we'll be fine." Basel carried Arnold to the house, up the marble steps and down the hall, past the gym, and into Arnold's room. Basel laid him down on his bed. He couldn't help being aroused, but he did not go further. He liked this job and would like to keep it longer. He trudged back to the barn to help,

Dru was sitting, quietly watching the 3D printer. The printer painstakingly moved back and forth. A bone was taking shape excruciatingly slow. This would be the right leg. Legs were much more complicated than ears. Legs had a lot of pieces. Tendons, muscles, bones, blood vessels.

The plan, at this point, was to print the bones and debone the puppy's leg and hope the rest would stay intact. "These bones will take at least a week to print. By then, we will know if the ears are gonna make it."

* * * * * * * * * * * *

Pierre was sitting in his rocking chair, drinking coffee. The postman walked up to his porch and handed him a stack of letters with a polite hello.

Pierre looked down and flipped through them. A new line of credit is extended to you! Cheerios are ten cents off! Electric bill was higher than expected. Probably because he left the a/c on all night.

He looked at the large brown envelope. He opened the biggest ones last. It was a silly old habit, but better to wade through the trash to get the prize. It simply had the toy store's address; no name on it. He looked at the top left corner of the envelope and froze. Jaspierre.

The envelope grew blurry as tears filled his eyes. She had found him. Severina was either not interested or dead. He was always expecting at some point she'd come back to get him. But the girl...

He never knew if she would. Kitten. That little kitten. He waited for his heart to settle a little. He drew in a breath.

Old memories bubbled up inside him; both the welcome and the unwelcome. He played it out in his head. She had figured out who he was because of the table. He had put hints in it. But not too many.

He thought about carving all the little planks. They told a story. A love story. About him and Severina. How they met. How they loved. How she... Well, it didn't scream, "tied in a basement," but it did say something. Paris. And it spoke of hope that things could get better.

He supposed they did get better. He was, after all, still alive. That had seemed like a question for so long. Would he even make it another year? And he somehow always did. He was unexpectedly let go by his tiny child. She had begged him to stay.

But Severina would have killed both of them. He brushed the tears off his cheeks and opened it. The first thing that fell out was his passport. It only had the one stamp to America in it. He frowned. Surely she didn't want him to travel.

The next one was a picture of him and Severina. Her naked breasts against his young skin awoke his older body. It was so messed up. But he would give it to her again if she let him. He was so exposed, sitting on the porch. He stepped inside the storefront and shut the glass door that had Pop's toys painted on the front. Hand carved wooden toys lined the shelves. His was one of the last handmade toy shops in the world, or so it seemed. He went back to his office and stared at her picture. She was so terrible, yet gorgeous. He never could decide if he loved her or hated her. Probably both at the same time.

He tore his eyes away and looked in the envelope again. More envelopes. He dumped them on his lap. It was strange to see his own handwriting. He flipped through them. Not even a word from Jaspierre. In fact, the only part that mentioned her was the return address. A sense of dread. Had she even sent it? Why no note?

He tore open the first letter he had written and read his short letter.

Hey, Pops,

I don't know how to tell you this. But I flew to America. I met a girl. She is fantastic. I'm going to convince her to marry me. I know you are gonna be upset. I am sorry I won't be able to take over for you, like we had discussed. But I am going to continue crafting toys. I'll be our American branch. Doesn't that sound great? I'll open my own Pop's Toys! All I need is a block of wood and the will to carve it, right?

I love you lots, and I'm gonna miss you terribly.

Pierre.

Pops was long dead. He tore opened the next one.

Hey, Pops,

I don't know if I have said this yet, but I love her. I love Severina. She has been through a lot though. She's not... well, she's not a great person. But I think she needs someone to love her, to show her how wonderful she is. I think her uncle molested her when she was younger. She seems like such a... hurt soul. I proposed. She said yes, but then she laughed at my ring and said she would only wear something more special than that. It hurt, but I can understand. She is a wealthy woman and wouldn't want the ring of a toymaker.

> *Anyway, I miss you more than I expected.*
> *Pierre*

It was strange to remember his attempt of a proposal. How she laughed. Two left.

> *Pops-*
> *I met her uncle. She has him tied up in the basement. I... I don't know what to say about it. It's confusing to me. She's been out in the barn a lot lately and explained to me she has been attempting surgery on animals. I... I don't know if I am safe here.*
> *Pierre*

The last letter was probably the saddest one.

> *Pops-*
> *I love her, but she is so screwed up. It's not safe here. I am gonna try to come home. She... I wish I could help her. She doesn't have to be like this. We could be so happy together if she would let us. See you soon.*
> *Pierre*

There were drops of blood on this one.

Chapter

Fourteen

Jaspierre stood in a brightly colored room covered with thick padded mats. On the back wall was a huge, shiny mirror. In her right hand, she held a long fencing sword. She had no real intention of learning fencing. But there were few people who taught combat swordsmanship. This particular type of fencing class was more free range and less fancy footwork. Her black t-shirt and tight yoga pants strained against her baby belly.

She did not take a class with a large group of people. That was beneath her. She hired a sole instructor for the day. "I would like to defend myself with a blade," she said. "The thing is, I have had plenty of this training before, but I don't have a sparring partner. So, I would just like to brush up on my skills."

"That's not exactly what we do here," he said. "We are not training for combat. Perhaps you mean martial arts or some other type of instructor?"

"Nonsense," she said, raising her blade and smacking him.

"Oh hey! I didn't want to say anything but, I don't think you're in any condition to swordfight," he said. She promptly smacked him again, harder.

"Fuck you." She raised her arm again, ready to hit him.

"Alright, let's go." He raised his own sword and smacked hers out of her hand immediately.

"Fuck!" she said, scrambling to grab her sword. Once it was within her fingertips, she spun with every intention of decapitating her sparring partner. But he was quicker than she, and knocked her sword loose once more.

"Are you sure you've been trained with a blade?" he said.

"Fuck you," she said, scrambling again for the second time after her sword. She grabbed the blade off the floor and wondered to herself if she was really this rusty. Or had she learned nothing by sparring with Marcy? Had she ever had any skills of the blade?

This time, she was more careful with her approach and managed to keep her blade in her hand. But after twenty minutes of his back and forth, and forth and back running across the room, swiping, smacking, and crashing blades, it was obvious to her that he could defeat her. Any day of the week, anytime he wanted. *Fuck*. She left the studio discouraged and pissed off. Was she good at anything anymore? She was having a fucking baby.

What was she supposed to do now? She couldn't defend herself against Dru or Arnold or Basel. She couldn't defend herself against a simple fucking stupid fencing instructor. Maybe she really didn't know shit. She sat in her car, her fingertips pressed to her skull, and she wondered what the fucking hell she should do. She did the same thing she always did when she was feeling like shit. Her tires squealed into the parking lot of her little bar.

She was still in her black yoga pants and her boring black t-shirt, but she had a change of clothes in the trunk. She snuck in the back and pulled on a sparkling silver dress, wig, and navy pumps. It was knee-length and already was almost too tight to wear across her belly. The fabric was stretched to its very limits. In this way, with this black short wig, long, sparkly silver dress, and dark blue pumps, she slipped into the bar.

"Hi, Thomas," she said. "What is there for fun today?" She could feel the tense, pissy attitude flare out of her mouth.

"Oh hey, you all right?" he said. "You need

a drink? Sound like you're having a bad day."

"I am having a fucking awful day. Can't drink, pregnant," she said. "What is there for fun today?" she repeated herself.

He stared at her, wondering curiously. Finally, he glanced around the room, considering, then looked back at her. "That man in the corner, in the suit, he's from out of town." He winked at Jaspierre, and then went back to his work. Jaspierre considered the fellow, and finally decided that instead of playing darts, she needed a bit more of a confidence booster.

It didn't take too long to convince the random stupid man to go outside for a little booty call. And he diced up just fine. She cut him, sliced him, stabbed him, and every other incantation she could do with the blade. He never stopped her; he couldn't stop her. She was fucking amazing. So why the fucking hell couldn't she beat a mother-fucking fencing instructor? Was it because she was pregnant?

CHAPTER

FIFTEEN

Jaspierre sat at her control center. The one large glass window in front of her stared into the large white maze. Ikali and Tessa were running around, and she kept moving the platform and sliding the walls, blocking them from the lone brown rabbit. Every time they'd get close, she'd shift the maze again. They were having a lot of fun.

Jaspierre couldn't stop thinking about that fencing instructor. What was it that made him so impossible to defeat? Who exactly had she murdered? Katie, but she hadn't seen it coming. In fact, in a fit of rage, she just rammed scissors in her back. She killed Russell, but he was injured and probably delusional. In fact, as he tried to protest, he was too weak to even slow her while she chopped off his head. And Baldy, well he – he just wasn't that hard to kill. Maybe she was not actually that good at using a sword?

She used to feel that she was good at it. She'd tussle with Marcy at least once a week. But maybe Marcy also sucked. Maybe Marcy was also terrible at sword fighting. And all those times she used her sword on Lucas? He never fought back. He just wanted to live. He didn't want to fight. It seemed like, perhaps, she was mistaken at her own skills. This troubled her greatly.

While she was contemplating, Tessa leapt up high over a wall. She tried to shift it quickly, but the serval was quicker than she was. The rabbit was quickly consumed. "Great game, guys." She grinned at her beautiful servals. It was a wonderful thing to have such gorgeous, talented pets.

Her big, swollen belly started kicking enthusiastically at her. This baby needed a mom who could protect it. It seemed she was unable to defend herself. She could barely swordfight anymore. She couldn't stop Dru from calling her stupid; he felt barely within her control. Just a few months earlier, if he had said such a thing to her, he would've been stabbed. Of course, if he fought back, maybe she'd be the one dead. She protectively rested her hands on the child growing inside her. Perhaps that was why she hadn't tried to kill him yet.

She really wanted Mother, that fierce, cold woman. Mother never hesitated; she would tell her what to do or even kill Dru herself. She wanted to give this brand-new child of hers a grandmother, a grandfather, or an actual father. But Lucas was dead. Mother was dead. Pierre was lost. The best she had was a ruppie. Maybe some things were better left undone, better left unmade. Maybe it was safer for this baby not to have Dru and Arnold and Basel in this house. But it was too late; it had already begun. And she wanted Mother to be proud. *It was her last chance.*

She scampered up the stairs, through the library, carefully pausing to click the fireplace shut and lock the door behind her. Her effort to avoid the three scary men in her house was successful. Quickly, she slipped up the last flight of stairs. These days, all she did was hide in the library or the maze or locked in her bedroom. She did not like these men. Her bedroom door was suspiciously open. She stepped inside to see Basel rummaging in her closet. Anger flared within her, and she pulled a long blade out of her bedpost.

The tip of the blade pressed into his back before he even knew she was there. "What the fuck are you doing in my room?" she said.

"I--um, I need a towel," he said.

She stared slowly at the big black man. Her heart practically thumped out of her chest. He was lying, and they both knew it. But she had to decide. Punish him? Fight him? Even with a blade aimed at his throat, he looked bigger than her. The baby in her belly flipped over, and she felt vulnerable instead of angry. The tip of the sword trembled in her fingertips. Would he be easily defeated like Baldy? He was on alert, staring at her, with a clenched fist, ready to hit her. Or was he like the fencing instructor? Her confidence had been shaken. "Get the fuck out of my room." She lowered the blade like a weakling. *Like a loser.*

"Whatever you say, boss." And he smiled a sick, twisted smile. The kind of smile of a man who knew he had just fucking won.

He left the room. *But she was so fucking mad.* She closed her eyes and counted to ten, then, when her heart had stopped pounding quite so hard, she slid the blade back into the serval carving. Time to get another fencing lesson. She needed to be a better version of herself in order to face these men. The bedroom lock clicked as she turned it. She paused. Didn't she always keep it locked? That fucker picked it. She made a phone call to her security firm, and they came and added additional security to her bedroom door. And she scheduled two sessions a week with the fencing instructor.

She might not be able to defend herself against these men yet. But their time would come.

CHAPTER

SIXTEEN

The baby fluttered a tiny kick within her big round belly. Time was passing and things had gotten better. Jaspierre knew Mother would have been insanely pleased. Work had been keeping her busy lately. She attended several board meetings, and the 3D printers were flying off the shelves. Their first foray into medical equipment sales was extremely profitable. Jaspierre even ordered a second one for herself. Printing two ears or legs, or whatever they needed simultaneously would speed the results and, hopefully, speed up the time in which experiments would end. Then she could kick out Dru, Arnold, and Basel. Printing bodies was hard and slow; a ruppie finally survived with both ears attached firmly. They had decent blood flow and looked adorable. Her own puppy with rabbit ears. Switching out the legs would be much harder, but having one puppy survive the first step was extremely encouraging. It was success.

Four more puppies had one ear take and one not. One printer set about creating ears while the other worked away at bones. At this rate, a viable ruppie would exist in a year. Jaspierre went off to more board meetings, while Dru walked back out to the barn.

Arnold and Basel were tending to the animals. Arnold filled each water bowl while Basel fed them and petted them. The printers squealed in little zippy spurts as they manufactured rabbit-shaped puppy parts. Dru checked on the latest two ear transplants. Both appeared to have taken well. He massaged them to increase the blood flow. The left one seemed healthy, and the right one seemed decent too. They didn't have fur on them, though. These ears were skin. Dru wasn't quite sure how to coax them to grow fur. It was there in the DNA if he could figure out how to unlock it. The trickiest parts of printing body parts wasn't making them the right shape, it was coaxing them to burst to life. He wasn't printing anything particularly difficult, like an organ. He kept all of the hearing parts from the puppy in his head.

At this point, they had lost thirty puppies. Basel was extremely good at finding more of them. Dru didn't know or care where he got them from, but he needed at least thirty more. The losses would go up as the bones in the legs were changed. Ears were simple in comparison. That was why they were such a good place to start.

Dru envisioned that soon there would be little 3-D printers in shady offices in the city where a doctor would print up bigger breasts inside old ones. Or print fuller cheeks, a straighter nose. Cosmetic surgery would be easier than ever; no more saline bags popping inside people. Print up a better shape with the proper DNA. Nothing to pop, nothing to fuss about. There could be a kiosk in every mall printing out parts as easily as custom t-shirts.

Not that Dru cared much. He had bigger, badder plans. *Imagine this; wake up and someone has printed and attached an elephant nose to yours.* Oh, the parts he could attach on the unwitting population. Freak shows would become popular again. Insanely popular.

He considered the time working on this ruppie to be experience for things yet to come. When this job was over, he would take his team and make his own mark on the world. Basel carried a small brown puppy to the operating table. "Hey, boss, these ears are done printing. We better get going."

"What fun," Dru said and scrubbed his hands. Arnold washed his own hands meticulously and the two of them began the operation.

Basel did not operate. It wasn't his thing.

He trudged back from the barn to the giant mansion, pausing to admire the bushes carved into cats. He thumped up the big marble steps and into the foyer. Gorgeous marble stairs spiraled up to the right, but he went left into the kitchen. He should start cooking or washing dishes. He kept thinking about Jaspierre. It had been at least a month or two and he still hadn't managed to dose her with a sedative. It was starting to grate on him. Usually, it was so easy to slip it in. She was cautious, wily even, that little lady.

He walked into her office. She had told them they couldn't be in there, but he wasn't one to follow rules. A massive wooden desk sat in the middle of the room. Each wall was covered in custom cut bookshelves. One of those ladders on wheels even sat on one shelf, like a library. There was a fireplace in this room. It was huge. Basel didn't even know they made fireplaces that big. It was bigger than his old bathroom. The sides of each fireplace had a carved statue of big cats. He ran his fingertips along the books, noting how dusty they were. Were they for show and she didn't know how to read? He cracked himself up and burst into laughter, leaning on the cat carving by the fireplace. There was a little click and the fireplace swung open. His seven-foot frame had to duck as he climbed down the stairs.

This was exciting. Dru would be jealous

Basel found it. Down here was a crisp, clean white room. There was one large observation window and a huge control panel. Several large monitors showed different angles into the room. There were three windows on the right the looked down into three individual rooms. Each of those rooms was empty and white, except for the metal rings on the back wall. They climbed up the walls in pairs. Strike that; two rooms were empty. One had a bed.

Directly in front of the console was a room easily as big as a football field. In it were white panels in all sorts of shapes. As he stared at them, they shifted into a new configuration. It appeared to be a maze. A rabbit hopped and scurried to a little fountain of water. It drank while a big cat leapt down. This cat was too big to be a house cat. It was Labrador-sized and had big ears. It had dots like a cheetah but also had stripes like a tiger. The cat raised its tail end into the air and crept closer to the rabbit. Just before it pounced, another one of those big cats leapt down on top of the rabbit. The rabbit let out a scream like a small child. It electrified Basel as he watched the pair chase each other and consume the rabbit.

He sat at the control panel and messed with the buttons. Two blue buttons blinked, and he started with those. Two glass doors opened on the left of the console under the big observation window. Ikali and Tessa both came charging out.

They were sick and tired of being locked down there.

Basel's eyes grew wide. This was a mistake. He let out these creatures. He froze by the console, hoping they wouldn't attack him. Tessa purred loudly and sat on his lap. Not vicious, at least. He picked her up and set her head on his shoulder as though she was a toddler, not a cat. He reached down and swiped Ikali off the floor and there he was with two cats in his arms. He needed to figure out what to do with them. He turned to stuff them back in the glass doors.

"You irritate the shit out of me," Jaspierre said. She stood there in high heels and a long suit. Her hair was long and curled down her back. "You must take me for a fool. You think I don't know you've been trying to dope me. You think I wouldn't notice you came down here? *You're* the fool." She reached for the control board and pressed a few buttons. The glass doors stayed open, but the fireplace swung shut.

Tessa and Ikali squirmed and clawed, painfully digging into Basel as he stood there dumbfounded. He tried to drop them both. Ikali hit the ground and snarled, biting his calf. Tessa held on for dear life, clinging her claws into his belly and shoulder. Basel hollered and tried to back up. Jaspierre opened a door behind him with the console. Her speed was remarkable and she charged him. He tripped backwards, sliding down a spiral staircase. He hit the ground hard, Tessa still clawing on him. She let out a hiss and leapt to the top of the staircase in one smooth movement. The door at the top of the staircase shut.

He stood alone in a hallway; it was white and smooth. Not a single door visible, not even the one at the top of the staircase he had just fallen down. He looked back and forth, trying to decide which way to run. A door appeared in the smooth hallway as it opened. Inside was a room with metal rings in pairs on the wall.

* * * * * * * * * * * *

The house was nearly ready. Chance had everything in place. He almost regretted the facial tattoo. What if she didn't like it? Of course she'd like it. She was Jaspierre. She loved her men rough and difficult. He figured she loved sex as much as he did. She had that Russell guy and that Lucas freak eating out of her hands. *Do you like it rough, Jaspierre?* Both of those men were roughed up. She'd go for his tattoo. It'd make her swoon.

Still, he wasn't quite ready to pick her up yet. He was a cop, though, so stakeouts weren't a big deal. Watching her from afar was his kind of flirting. He sat in the old red truck he found at the cabin. He wore a baseball cap and thick, dark sunglasses. They almost made him giggle; wasn't this a standard perp look? *Oh, you'll never notice me now that I have sunglasses!* He almost roared with laughter. It was funny because it was *true*. It actually worked! Sunglasses make a person's face fade into the background, even a memorable face like his own. He had considered getting the kind of makeup girls used to make their skin look less ugly. But in the end, he didn't want to smear that goop on him. He patiently sat. She'd have to show up to work soon. The truck was already littered with fast food trash and porn magazines. And beer cans and a vodka bottle. *Come on, you slutty hussy, shake your tail for me a little. Let's fall in love all over again.* She drove up and the valet took her keys. She stepped out of the car, and there she was. Her heels were tall and a glittery red. Her skirt was long, dark blue, and hugged her ass just perfect. Her round breasts threatened to burst out of her shirt.

 The wig she wore today was the long, brown curled one. She always wore one to work. Her work-self had long hair. He got it. His work-self wore a badge and it was practically the same thing. *You gotta look a certain way to make the pay.* His plan to observe her flickered, as he had to hold back the urge to take her. Go snatch her up and take her home and show her all the things he'd made for her. Have babies and grow old living off the land. It'd be magnificent. They'd have a family. She needed a family as badly as he did. Her mom was gone, her dads were gone, and she didn't have a soul. He was about the same. His dad shot his mom when he was five or six. His dad blew his own head off, and Chance stayed with his aunt. That was how he met Jasp, living with his aunt Liddy. She cleaned that big old house of hers.

But after he got tossed into foster care, he hadn't seen Jasp much after that. He never let go of her in his heart, though. Now he was jobless, but living off the land wasn't that big of a deal. The hunting was sure fun. *Pow pow, and the brains 'splode.* It never lost its charm.

Charming her would be important this time around. He botched it last time by killing that chick tied on the kitchen table. That old lady. The "it's not cheating if she's dead" line only went so far. He had to get her a ring this time and make it real. *Jaspierre, girl, get ready for the proposal of your dreams.*

She had long gone inside. *Damn. Should pay closer attention.* He almost started the car and drove off to sit in the cabin again. Watch some porn, think about their kids.

But then he saw it. A sparkle.

A thin, tit-less woman in a red dress and obnoxiously tall heels was strutting down the sidewalk. Her ring finger sparkled bright as sunshine. Didn't he just think he needed a ring? It had to be a pretty damn good ring for it to sparkle all the way across the street like that. She wore a large hat with a dark veil pulled over her eyes. She was walking with purpose, one foot confidently clicking after the other. The heels slowed her down just a smidge. It wouldn't be difficult at all to catch up with her. He hopped out of the truck and onto the sidewalk, pulling his baseball cap down low, and locking the door. A moment or two later, he was across the street, following at a safe distance. There would be a moment, soon, where she would pause at an alley, or head to her apartment, or step into a quiet part of the city. He watched for that moment; the moment when there wouldn't be anyone to witness him.

He'd follow her until he got it off her finger, or got her finger off. Didn't matter which.

Of course, if he got her finger off, he'd have to take her home...

* * * * * * * * * * *

Jessi rapped on Edward's desk. "Hey, we didn't find the boy."

"Shit," Edward said. "Did you find anything? Do we even have a hint where he is?"

"I don't know. I thought maybe you'd want to ride with me for another look," she said. "I know the odds aren't good, but I'm tired of sitting uselessly at my desk."

"You know what? I'd be happy to leave my

desk right now. I haven't gotten anywhere on this case. I've been calling people, but they won't call back. Chance has vanished. I don't even know where to go from here. A break would do me some good," he said, and he grabbed his coat. And they were back in her squad car.

As they were winding up the long, two-lane road, he tried to peer through the tightly pressed together pine trees. He couldn't see much. "You really think he's wandering around out there?"

"We found his footprints the day after we were all up there looking in the cabin. I am just sure if we can figure out where to search, we would find them. But that big search team had no luck, so the odds are against us." She drove with a concerned look on her face, eyes scanning back and forth, back and forth. He knew she was thinking about the scared eight-year-old, Peter Mirabella. Was he hungry? He was most certainly scared. Was he cold? The fall weather had gotten nippy. An eight-year-old boy couldn't survive long in the woods alone with no adults. Or worse, he still had an adult. A man accused of child molestation. He hoped they weren't together.

But maybe Peter would be better off with Jack than without him. A kid could die out there alone in the woods. She slowed as they turned around a tight corner. "What was that?" he said.

"I didn't see it," she said. "What do you

think it was?"

"I think we should turn around. Try to be quiet about it, though." His eyes scanned the left half of the road and, as she turned, he stared on the right half. His eyes never left the tree line, tightly packed as it was. She crept forward quietly, watching the road and glancing to the right.

"What do you think you...?"

"Holy fucking cow," he interrupted. "Holy fucking cow. Do you see that?" There was a break in the trees where a narrow dirt driveway led to a small, mostly rotted cabin. It looked like an ancient home; one of the sides slanted in and the roof seemed to be just about to teeter off. A dash of smoke came from the chimney, or what was left of the chimney. The bricks were scattered on top of the slanted roof. Standing at the front door was Jack. He appeared to be trying to prop up the front door to stop it from falling. As they sat there and watched in mute amazement, he dropped the door and it fell flat on the ground. He picked it back up, ready to wrestle it back into place.

"Call it in, and let's catch him," he said. She nodded. She spoke into her radio quickly, and they both hopped out of their seats with guns drawn and advanced on Jack.

"Put your hands up," she said.

"I ain't done nothing." The door was in his hands. He did not put his hands up.

"I said put your hands up. Drop the door and put your hands up," Jessi said.

Jack held the door up, using it as a shield. He backed into the little falling-apart cabin. "Don't you come any closer. I will fuck this kid up."

Edward glanced at Jessi; did she want him to go around the back or the front? She looked over and caught his eye. She nodded to the front as she strode around the building to the back. He kept his gun on the door and watched as Jack propped the door up in place.

"Jack, you aren't going to hurt that boy. Not on my watch. We've got you surrounded. There's nowhere you can go," he said. "Come out with your hands up."

"I ain't coming out. Not with my hands up. Not with my hands down. I ain't coming out," he shouted, the sound muffled from behind the door.

"Look, Jack, we've got you caught. What do you think is going to happen next? Nothing good, that's for sure. Nothing good at all. You want a bullet in your brain? Or do you want to settle this civilly?" Edward said. He was hoping that all this chitchat nonsense would give Jessi time to get inside. Take him from behind. A nice, simple, altercation-free arrest. And with any luck, Peter would be sitting inside, right as rain.

"You better go away. I ain't kidding. I am gonna screw this kid up. I am going to do it!" Jack said. "You can't see me. But I got my gun aimed at him right now."

"Jack, I can see your fingertips holding up that door."

"Fuck you. You can't see shit."

"Jack. You better give it up. We've got you surrounded. Let Peter go. Let..." He was interrupted by a large crash. Four gunshots were fired. Edward charged at the door, busting into the little shack. The door clattered to the floor, on top of Jessi. She was bleeding. She let out a yelp when the door smashed onto her fallen body.

"Look out!" she shouted.

He turned, but it was too late. Jack had his gun drawn and clicked the trigger. The revolver was pointed directly into Edward's gut. The gun clicked, but nothing happened. Jack shook it and clicked again. Before Edward could process that the gun was misfiring, Jack turned and looked into the barrel. It was at this moment that the bullet finally fired.

CHAPTER

SEVENTEEN

"You can step in or I can drag your unconscious body in. I don't give a shit which," Jaspierre spoke into the microphone on the headset she was wearing. She watched the screen of the empty room. Basel's huge black figure stuck his head in. She resisted the urge to snap the razor-lined door shut, decapitating him.

He paused and then looked back around the hall. Everything was a crisp, clean white. There were no visible doors; even the one at the top of the metal spiral staircase had vanished. He didn't have much of a choice. Besides, if he obeyed her, he probably would get a lighter sentence. That was how the world was supposed to work, at least. *Do as you're told and you get to keep your skin.* He stepped into the white room with the rings in pairs up the back wall.

The room was otherwise white; the walls were smooth. Once he stepped inside, the doorway behind him disappeared. Now he was in a white smooth box.

"Let's be quick about this. Do you see the light?" she said. He looked around the room and there was a red dot flickering on the wall. It was midway from one wall to the other and higher than his belly button. "Press your hand on it for twenty seconds. This is the only time I am going to show you where it is. Memorize it."

He held his hand on the wall and counted to twenty. A small door slid open. A toilet and a little sink were revealed. They both stuck out towards the room. If Basel sat, his feet would be well into this white box. He turned back and tried to remember where the dot was. *Fuck, he already forgot.*

"Hey, I am sorry, you know? I didn't know you had pets down here. I got curious. I was trying to put them back when you walked in, right? So if you think about it: no harm, no foul." Basel spoke to the room. Nobody answered. Had she left? The bathroom door slid shut, and the wall was blank again.

"I haven't ever tried to dose you with anything!" he lied. "I'd never do that, especially since you're pregnant. Yeah, it's not a well-kept secret at this point. I'm not a baby killer." He counted his steps to the midpoint of the room. The dot of light had to be around here. He slid his hand on the wall. *Shit.* He had to hold it still.

Good thing he didn't have diarrhea; he'd shit himself before he got the door opened.

"So, if you're still up there, let me know. We can work this out. It's not a big deal." He paused, hand on the wall, and listened for her answer.

Silence.

"Fuck, can you show me the toilet again?" He moved his hand and waited. He'd have to mark it or he was never gonna be able to piss. How long did she plan on keeping him down here? Pleading began to fade into rage. "Why the fuck are you leaving me down here? Talk to me! What the fuck do you want!" He punched the wall and his bone cracked under the hit. "Goddamn, I broke my hand! I broke my fucking hand. Let me out so I can get it fixed. This is fucking shit!"

Eventually, he slept. When he woke, he had to pee, and he spent at least an hour trying to get the door open. When he found the spot, he tore a fingernail loose a little and smeared the spot with blood. Fuck hunting for the door all the damn time.

* * * * * * * * * * *

Peter was still missing. Jessi was in the hospital. Jack was dead. Edward sat at his desk with his head held by his fingertips. They didn't expect Jessi to make it; she'd been shot in the chest two times. Edward couldn't get over that he could see the fingertips of Jack holding the door. How the hell had he shot her? They didn't find Peter. He was probably roaming the woods.

If Jack hadn't shot himself in the face, they could question him. They could've given him a lighter sentence in return for the boy. Any details would be helpful. Had the boy ever been in that shack? Had the boy shot Jessi? Had he escaped and given Jack a run for his money? A tidal wave of volunteers were wandering the woods like a flash flood crashing between the trees. He hoped they would find Peter, but it seemed like his luck was starting to run out.

He was thinking about all these things: Jessi in the hospital, Jack dead, and Peter lost and alone in the woods. His mind was a flurry of worried thoughts. He massaged his temples slowly, mindlessly staring at his desk. Suddenly, he realized there was a new report. The beheaded man that had been found in the woods near Chance's burned home; he wasn't Chance. His name was Russell Tyler Holmes. He was twenty-two, had pasty red hair and green eyes. He had been working as grocery bagger when he went missing. His parents' names were Dolores and Michael. He drove a yellow VW bug, which was recently towed from a Chinese food restaurant. Russell appeared to be a real flaky guy; he'd applied to at least seven different colleges in the last three years. The kid had taken out many a student loan, but he'd never completed any degree. In fact, by the look of his transcripts, he'd flunked out of all of the colleges that he'd attended. Before Edward called the parents, he decided he'd call the grocery store and see the last time he went to work.

"Hello. Is the manager available?"

"This is her. What do you need?"

"Can you tell me, what was the last day Russell Tyler Holmes showed up to work?"

"Oh gee, Russell hasn't been around for a while. Couple months at least? He just stopped showing up to work. Lots of people do that. Bagging groceries isn't exactly a career type job. People don't stick around."

"I think you have misunderstood me. My name is Edward Darbonne. I'm a detective. I'm trying to figure out the last time anyone saw Russell.. Do you know exactly which day he stopped working?" Edward asked. As soon as she said the date, he sucked in all his air. It was just a week before the fire. Russell, just like the others, had his toes snipped off. His arm had been broken. In addition to that, he had been beheaded.

I am back on the case. The body wasn't Chance.

So far, at the cop's house, Helen had her toes snipped off and her arm broken. Russell had his toes snipped off, his arm broken, and he was beheaded just outside the home. The third victim, John Doe, had his toes snipped off, then allowed to heal. His arm wasn't broken, and he wasn't beheaded, but he had been shot in the face. When Edward spoke with Russell's parents, he found out the reason why they hadn't reported him as missing was because they didn't know. They had had a very strained relationship.

Helen had no contents in her stomach at the time of death.

Russell's last meal was Gatorade, granola bars, and cookies. Edward rubbed his hands together and sat at his desk. He was making actual progress in this case.

Each clue gave him new leads and new questions. Could his last meal have been at Chance's house? Did Jack give Peter to Chance? He hopped in his car and drove back down there to check the burned remains of the pantry. The pantry hadn't burned quite as badly as the rest of the house. The door had been closed, and the firefighters had gotten there before it had been fully consumed by flames. It was still burnt up; the floor was dark and soot-covered. But the shelves had melted Gatorade bottles, and it seemed granola bars and cookies and crackers were plenty. Best guess, Russell had been here. He took off right before the fire; hell, maybe he lit the fire. He managed to get a half mile down the road before Chance caught him and decapitated him. A large task force of cops and volunteers walked the woods around the house, but they didn't find any other bodies. Either Chance had hid them better or there weren't any more in the woods.

Chance, where the hell are you? Do you have Peter?

JASPIERRE'S DESCENT

CHAPTER

EIGHTEEN

Jasp was in her black Lexus, driving down the road at a fast clip. She was furious Basel was locked down in her basement. How dare he? How *dare* he touch her cats and go through her things. She couldn't stand it. She barely slept, tossing and turning around her bulging pregnant belly. The baby kicked repeatedly and she had nightmare after nightmare of Chance trying to cut it out of her belly. *Chance was dead. Get the hell out of my dreams.*

Dru and Arnold asked her if she had seen Basel and she just walked right out of the house. Hopped in her Lexus and went for a drive. *Life sucked.* She couldn't find her dad. They hadn't made a ruppie. Chance was haunting her dreams. Basel would kill her cats. Everything led back to Lucas. He was supposed to be holding her hand and having this baby together. Chance had stolen from her. She only met Lucas because of her cats.

Those were his rooms. His cells. That was their place. Basel was tainting it with his stupid ugly body. He was ruining everything. She was gonna kill him. But not down there; she didn't need any more memories of men down in her cells. That time of life was over.

Chance still haunted her thoughts. Almost more than Lucas. He had been such a scary man. Why couldn't he be obsessed with someone else? Perhaps if she had been able to love him back, things would have gone differently. Then Lucas would be alive. Even killing that stupid bald man hadn't helped. She still constantly watched over her shoulder. He was dead. She burned him in that house. She did it. He was dead. Time to move on.

She turned down the long country road. The gold ring with the little white stone caught her eye. What would Pierre think of her now? In a few minutes, she'd be driving past Chance's house, past the house where Lucas was shot to death. The burned crumbled remains of his house. The same place where Lucas exploded over and over again on her face. She wasn't even sure why she wanted to go there so badly. That memory never stopped replaying. She pushed the gas, ready to fly past the burnt building. Tears streaked her face as the charred roof came into view.

She braked. If she looked inside, perhaps

the memories would have less of a grip on her soul. Her brakes squealed and her car slid as she parked in the driveway. Her vision blurred as tears filled her eyes. She popped open the door and snapped it shut. Police tape wrapped around the house. She peeked in the broken windows. There was the crisp, charred couch. He wasn't sitting on it anymore. *It's really over. Chance is truly dead. Lucas is completely gone. It's over.*

"What are you doing?" A booming male voice carried out to her ears.

Flustered, her face flushed red. Was it obvious she was crying? "I saw all the police tape. I got curious."

"I'm Detective Edward Darbonne. Do you know who used to live here?"

"Um, no. A cop? I drive by occasionally. I saw a cop car here a few times. I didn't realize you guys were still investigating. I was just curious. I'll head out." Jaspierre smiled briefly and walked towards her car.

"What was your name?"

"Danielle," she said with the smooth ease of someone who lies about who they are on a regular basis. She regretted leaving the house without a wig. She had sunglasses on, at least. She reached out her hand and shook his. His hand was warm and firm.

"Do you know anything about the fire?" he asked, sizing her up.

"Not a thing. I'm sorry I bothered you." She walked to her black Lexus.

Edward stared at her car. "You drive a Lexus?" She nodded, but the hairs on the back of her neck stood up. She needed to leave and fast. Her door opened and her ass hit the seat.

"See you around," she said, and the door snapped shut. The car whirred to life and she drove off. *Fuck. Why did he care about my Lexus?*

* * * * * * * * * * * *

He had already taken down her plates. This Lexus had plates that were liars. This was *the* Lexus. The plate-stealing Lexus. He'd bet his badge on it. By the time he finished running her plates, she was long gone.

Edward had never considered Chance's partner was *alive* or a *female*. But that chick knew something. Many things, likely. He had hopped in his car and tried to catch up with her. He planned to pull her over for speeding and take her in. Then he could fingerprint her and properly question her. She knew Chance; she probably knew where he was right this moment. She was the connection. *She had the Lexus.* Her plates came up as a yellow VW bug owned by a man named Charles McFallen. Somehow, he didn't think they were stolen; it looked like she had made her own plates. Now he had to find her. He searched through everything he knew about Chance to find a woman he might have had contact with and not killed her.

Meanwhile, Jaspierre took her car in to be painted. It went from black to canary yellow. She made sure they removed the Lexus symbols when they painted. She replaced them with Mercedes-Benz logos. *Like anyone would know it was a Lexus now.* Fear was racing through her. What did that cop know about her? She considered dumping the car, but it seemed to be a poor choice. Better to hide it in plain sight. She parked it in her garage with all her other cars. It was a shame; that Lexus was one of her favorites to drive. Now it would sit, like a cloth-covered paperweight. That car wouldn't see the light of day for a long time. She had proper plates put on it too. She went out and bought a new silver Honda minivan with cash under one of her fake names. Time for a new favorite; besides, she was going to be a mommy.

JASPIERRE'S DESCENT

CHAPTER

NINETEEN

Basel had been missing for a few days now. Dru wasn't sure if Jaspierre had run a sword through him, like that poor man called Russell who had been roasted in the fireplace, or if he had disappeared for another reason. Either way, he didn't care. Arnold and he did the bulk of the work. Basel cooked the meals. Microwaved food would have to do for now.

Basel missing did prove to be problematic, in a more pertinent way. He was the man who found the puppies. What would they do when they ran out? Arnold was excellent with the patients. Four puppies had undergone successful ear transplants at this point. The first printed bone transplant had gone poorly. Dru didn't know enough about how to attach muscles and tendons, and removing the first leg bone had killed the puppy. His second attempt had gone much better. The dog couldn't walk or move his foot, but he didn't die. *Improvement.* He read several medical studies on hip transplants and he thought he knew how to adjust it. The third attempt went even better than the first two. This leg had weak movement. Jaspierre hadn't specified if the legs needed to be fully functional, so Dru considered this success enough. As he traded out bones for the four viable puppies, he hoped to make improvements and at least one of them would be able to... hop. Or walk. Didn't matter to him. The point was to look like a mashup, not to have a puppy eat carrots.

Nearly fifty puppies had died during these experiments, but progress was being made at a rapid pace. More puppies, more progress. Some dogs just didn't have the constitution for the surgeries. Ten more puppies were in various states of experimentation, with one ear transplanted and the other ear dead, or not yet transplanted. Three of those puppies had undergone different leg surgeries. Most of these were exploratory so Dru could learn faster. Arnold was catching on. Because ears were so much faster to print than bones, Arnold had even successfully attached one on his own. Progress was a beautiful thing. If one puppy healed well, they could start on the second leg and they would have to chop the tail, and the first ruppie would be complete. It would be the official prototype, and they could improve functionality. Jaspierre would be delighted to hear this news.

Dru thought about Jaspierre. She was definitely pregnant. He liked that she had given him this opportunity to work for her, but he didn't like that he had no real way to control her. Basel and Arnold fell into place. They both preferred and respected Dru as the boss. Jaspierre did not. Jasp seemed to think she was the boss. Yes, it was *her* plan to build a ruppie – *her money, her house* – but he daydreamed more and more often about killing her and taking over her home as his own. How hard would it be to be her sole inheritor? Just a few slips of paper. Or, if convincing proved too difficult, then he could forge those documents, or he would bend her to his will another way. Men like Dru didn't love other people, but Jasp would learn to love him. Then they'd marry, and he'd control her assets. Then he could slit her throat if needed, depending on the circumstances. Well, it was an easy approach worth trying. Besides, weren't pregnant women desperate to have a man by their side?

Dru stood in the barn and massaged the rabbit ear on the puppy. With Basel gone, they did have a shortage of puppies. They had ten left to experiment on before they had to go find more. It wasn't too hard to buy them from puppy mills, and he probably could buy a handful of bitches and a male and make 'em himself. He had no patience for birthing puppies, though. Waiting for births created a supply and demand problem anyway. Then, to top that off, the puppies would have to grow to a surgery-able size. The sweet spot was right around three months old. They would be just past weaning, and yet still about to grow in giant spurts. Growth was important. Children heal so much faster than adults because of this intense growth. Puppies were the same. If the rabbit-shaped ears, legs, and tails had adhered by month four, his theory was the puppy could still easily learn to walk or hop, whichever it chose. And grow. These pieces being printed could grow and change with the puppy's body. At least, they were supposed to.

Jaspierre opened the door and waved at Dru. "Hey! How's it going? Are we getting close yet?"

"Hello, good looking. Yes, we're doing great," Dru said. Maybe that was laying it on a little thick.

Jaspierre wrinkled her forehead. "Uh... okay...." She coughed. "Okay. So show me what you've got."

Dru walked her to the top three puppies. "This one here is A2; he's a lab mix. Both of his ears have transplanted well. I don't know if they will ever grow fur, but they do seem to stand up like a proper rabbit's ears." The chocolate-colored dog had pale-skinned rabbit ears perked up out of its head. "He also has had the bones transferred on his back right leg, and so far, he has tolerated that well. He's not attempting to walk on it at all, but that's to be expected. It is likely he'll be lame for at least a while when the other back leg is transferred. If you'll look here at the skeleton of a rabbit, the biggest problem we will be encountering is a rabbit's spine curves downwards to its tail, placing the hip joint at the floor. Dogs, on the other hand, have a straighter spine, and their hip joint is up by their tails in the air. Even though we can change the physical shape of the leg, the spine itself is going to have to curve to the proper shape.

"To plan ahead for this, we have already started spine training the dogs with a harness six hours a day. Basically, we ratchet the spine into the bent shape we need and leave them like that. It appears to be working, as you notice A2 already has developed a significant curve compared to a regular dog."

Jaspierre nodded. A2 licked her fingers and seemed to be in a pleasant mood. "Have you been making sure they are socialized? Pain monitored so they aren't uncomfortable? I'd hate to fulfill my mother's dreams and have it be a wild, rabid creature." Of course, that would probably have pleased Mother considerably; an attack ruppie.

Dru took Jasp's hand and led her to the next cage. He said, "Of course they are tame. We are careful to make the transition as comfortable as possible for them. Is the baby kicking?"

Jaspierre released his hand and held her belly. Her little one squirmed within her. "Just a little. What is this one?"

Dru stood behind her and slid his hand to hers, the little kicks thumping through her skin. "May I?"

She grew flustered and stepped away. Red heat flew to her face. What was this? "Just the puppies," she said with a snap.

He backed off. Perhaps tonight she wouldn't fall for him, but soon. He had to tone it down a little. "This is B5. She's a smaller dog, if you notice. A terrier, I believe. Both her ear transplants have gone remarkably well. She is about to have her back right leg done. The printing is finished this afternoon. She is in remarkably good health and handled the ear transplants better than any other dog yet. I have high hopes for her recovery."

"And this is C12. He is a Spaniel. He is a medium-sized dog. His ear transplants have gone well also and he has had both back legs done. At this point, he is completely lame. He generally drags himself around by his front two feet. He hasn't rejected the legs, and that is the important part. His spine, if you see, is curving much slower than we would expect, so it is difficult for his hips to operate the new legs. We have been spine training him for a maximum of twelve hours a day in the hopes of speeding it up. He has physical therapy every three hours to increase blood flow and improve the strength of the legs. He almost looks like your mother's vision."

Jaspierre caressed her huge baby belly and stared at C12. The fleshy pointed ears were beautiful against the dark fur. His legs did look rabbit-ish, but the way he sprawled with them made it difficult to see what they would look like when he walked or hopped. "Very good. Thank you for your efforts on this." She walked back to the house wondering, *Would Mother finally be happy?*

* * * * * * * * * * * *

Chance sat in the red truck, chomping down chips. He stared into the binoculars and waited for her car to show up. He had been waiting a couple of hours and was considering heading home and trying again tomorrow. *Come along, Jaspierre, with your big round titties leading your bouncy ass around. Let's go, little lady. I would love to see your face. It's the love of your life waiting for you. Always for you. Only for you.* The skinny chick in the red dress had already been disposed of. When he meant he was waiting for Jasp and only for Jasp, he meant waiting to have babies with her. Besides, he was pretty sure it wasn't cheating if the lady was dead. Obviously, he couldn't suddenly become celibate just because he loved Jaspierre.

He belched and chugged his beer can. The stupid foam cover he had slid on it to hide the alcoholic contents to anyone passing by was sliding around uncomfortably. As he started to adjust it, he noticed for the first time his arms had grown bigger. The pants he wore tightened around his waist. All the weight that fell off him from the full body burns had been building back up. His arms and back were stronger than they had been in years. Digging out the cellar had done him good. The sun was shining, and he was almost ready to pick her up and take her home. A few more supply runs and it would be time. Today, he wanted to lay eyes on her.

Come along, Jaspierre. Little bit of eye candy for your big man.

She drove up in a dark pink Corvette, tossing the keys to the valet. It was warm today and she wasn't wearing a coat. Her dress hugged her ass. She turned to wave at the valet and Chance spit his beer. *Holy shit.* He stepped out of the truck and walked down the sidewalk to her, his heart pounding. *Holy fucking shit.*

She turned and he could see clearer. Her blood-red dress stretched tight against her belly. Her *pregnant* belly. They were fucking pregnant! He threw his hat and sunglasses as he stormed into traffic to her. How could she have kept this from him? They were having their first-born child and she hadn't even told him. A car honked and swerved around the angry man. Jaspierre turned around and her eyes grew wide. One hand protectively covered her stomach.

Chance held his hands out as if to hug her, still standing in the street. Happy tears ran. "Pregnant!" he shouted. The sun shone brightly through the clouds for a moment. Jaspierre stood frozen, one hand holding her lips, the other holding her belly.

A black car honked repeatedly, brakes squealing, and smashed into Chance. He rolled up onto the windshield, crushing it with his large body. Traffic squealed and braked, swerving around them. Chance lay on the hood, his head throbbing. He was gonna be a dad even sooner than he thought. He caught his breath. Drivers crawled out of vehicles, asking each other if they were okay. A crowd formed around the man on the hood. Chance rolled off the vehicle, taking his time. His chest hurt like hell. He staggered to his feet.

"Hey, dude, you gotta sit down. You've been in an accident. You're in shock." A man grabbed Chance's arm. Chance shot him in the belly. People screamed and ran.

"I'm gonna be a motherfucking father," Chance whispered to himself as he limped to his car, waving his gun at anyone who looked at him.

"A mother-fucking father." He climbed into the truck.

"We're having a baby!" He punched the ceiling of the truck and pressed the gas, squealing away.

CHAPTER

TWENTY

The room was spinning. Jaspierre's blood rushed to her head. A deep throbbing in her temples grew to unrelenting thumps. She was standing in the foyer of her office building. Someone was asking her something, but her ears couldn't make the sounds into words. *Chance.* This was a nightmare. A vision or hallucination. He was hideous. His face was covered in gnarled scars from the burns. They were exaggerated, as if he had drawn on them to make them more graphic.

More terrifying.

He was charging across traffic when the car hit him. The tires squealed.

Her hands trembled, heart beating faster and faster. Air couldn't make its way into her lungs. She was gasping. The secretary grabbed her elbow and tried to pull her to a chair. "I think you're having a panic attack..." she whispered in

Jaspierre's ear.

Jasp doubled over as pain filled her core. Her belly grew tight as a vise crushing her.

"Jaspierre? Are you okay?" The lady kept talking. *Shut up shut up.* Jaspierre grasped for her incoherent thoughts to come back together. She could hear sirens. That couldn't have been Chance.

Her stomach tightened again and Jasp hurled. A steady ache in her belly pushed harder and harder. "I think you're in labor!" The secretary with her stupid yapping yapper. She placed her hand on the offending belly and watched the time. "You're only five minutes apart. Time for the hospital. Do you need me to call the father?"

Jaspierre mentally severed her head. *Leave me alone. I'm trying to think!* Lucas was dead. *Chance was alive.* The valet pulled up with her pink Corvette and she climbed into the passenger seat.

Did Chance yell she was pregnant?

* * * * * * * * * * * *

Chance spent the rest of the day sleeping in the cabin. At around midnight, he awoke. His body ached from head to toe. He took a handful of whichever painkiller was sitting in the medicine cabinet and washed it down with a beer. He had never felt so alive. His ribs were bruised and broken, and his left buttocks was purple and sore. He'd have to heal up a bit. Jasp shouldn't have to see him like this on their honeymoon.

That said, he couldn't stop thinking about her. Her big round baby belly. *Oh god, she'd have milk soon.* He was so aroused, he thought about getting him a woman to get him through the next week or two. A warm-bodied sex toy. He spent an hour getting off so he could concentrate on a plan.

Afterwards, he just wanted more. His body hurt like hell and all he wanted was to see his baby-making mama. He could at least send her a present. Even though he wasn't in good enough shape to physically go down there and bring her back and bang her until she couldn't move...

No, that wasn't right. He wanted her to keep moving. Bang her until he was satisfied, not dead. Corpses couldn't have babies or make milk. It would be fun to learn to hold back. From inside the freezer, he took out the blue Tiffany box and packed it in a cooler with ice. He drove down to the grocery store and bought a small piece of dry ice. He'd hate for it to thaw before she saw it. He put the dry ice in the blue tissue and took his time arranging it. Then he closed it up, sealed it with tape, and stopped by the florist.

"What's the biggest bouquet you've got?" He grinned, his tattooed scars snarling on his face.

"It's $250; it's mostly roses. Pretty big, though, for a funeral centerpiece," the lady behind the counter said. She stepped backwards from the counter, instinctively afraid.

"That sounds perfect. Make me one. I'll take it right now."

"Oh, um, most of these are pre-ordered. It'll take me an hour to make it," she said nervously.

He stared at her body, wondering if she'd ever made milk. "I'll be back." He stepped out and walked down the street to a little donut shop. He sat with a cup of black coffee. It was nice to be out in full glory today. Sitting in the corner of the coffee booth, watching the world cringe when they looked at him. He sat and watched as time flew by. He stepped out of the shop to leave when he saw his red truck being towed. *Fucking fuck fuckers.*

A cop stood on the side of the street, talking to the people around him. Chance slipped into the flower shop, flipped the sign to closed, and locked the door. The lady at the counter came from the back room.

"Hey, are my flowers done?"

"Almost," she said nervously.

"Can I come back and watch you do the last bit?" he said with a boyish grin.

"No, customers can't come back there."

"Pretty please?" He stepped forward, and she cringed and stepped backwards.

"No." She could say it all she wanted. He

needed to hide out for an hour or two until the cop left. Besides, she was warm and could keep him busy that long. She whimpered as he dragged her into the back.

* * * * * * * * * * * *

Pierre handed the ticket to the teller. He was pale and terrified. He had made his decision, but he didn't feel good about it. He got on the airplane and sat in his seat. Next to him was a sullen, sleeping teenager. Thank goodness he wouldn't have to make small talk.

He stared at his hands as he sat, waiting for the plane to take off. He was missing the ring finger on his left hand. The tips of both pinkies had been amputated, and the tip of his right ring finger was missing. He didn't miss them much anymore, even though they never functioned as well as they should. But flying in a plane made him remember.

When he flew home all those years ago, all his fingers were still on him. The tips were black, and the ring finger on his left hand was completely dead. He wore gloves. That finger fell off his hand before the flight even landed. *Rejected.* He rejected the fingers she had put on his hands. After he talked with his pop, they went to the hospital. The doctor insisted on amputating the ruined pieces of his hands. Jasper's hairy skin patched into his was healthy in many places, so they left it. They carefully replaced the rotting pieces with skin grafts. *The rejected.*

Before he purchased his ticket he finally sat down at the computer and allowed himself to search. The articles he had found said she had been missing. That Jaspierre was alone and Severina was missing. Not dead, *missing.* He lingered on that thought over and over again. Missing. *Not dead.*

Was the girl as broken as he was? He'd know in about fifteen hours.

* * * * * * * * * * * *

Edward called the hospital to check on Jessi, but he was too late. She was already dead. Jack's fucking shots had killed her. And for what? Peter was still missing. Chance hadn't yet been found. What had Jessi traded her life for?

He sat at his desk discouraged, rubbing his temples with his fingertips. Jessi was a good person; she didn't deserve this. This felt like his fucking fault. He wanted to find that kid, find Jack, find Chance. If they hadn't gone chasing after Jack, maybe Peter would not have been snatched. If they hadn't gone chasing after Jack, he wouldn't have killed Jessi.

If they had found Peter, then at least it would seem like she died an honorable death saving a kid. But they hadn't found Peter; he was lost forever in the woods. Or already sold as a sex slave, or some other terrible fate. They couldn't find the kid, Jack was dead, Jessi was dead. Where was the justice? *Chance might have murdered his stepmother. Jack had probably molested Chance. Chance had killed people.* These were all things he knew, but not things he could use, unless he found the bastard.

And that kid. He couldn't imagine what it was like to be lost in the woods alone. A small, terrified child, stolen from his family, and then lost. Or sold, or locked up, or left. He hoped his imagination of the most terrible, frightening things that this boy could have had happen to him were the worse than any real event happening to him. *Who fucking knew?*

Jessi was dead.

JASPIERRE'S DESCENT

CHAPTER

TWENTY-ONE

Jaspierre lay in her hospital bed. Contraction after contraction pulsed through her body. They were monitoring her, but this was the worst time to have a baby. The absolute worst.

That couldn't have been Chance. Chance was dead. She'd poured the fuel, lit the match, and heard his screams. *He was dead, dammit.* She couldn't allow her hormone-fueled fears to rule her mind. It was a hallucination. Chance was dead.

Nothing could go right for Jaspierre. She didn't find Father; she might finish Mother's work, but letting Dru in the house was a becoming a huge problem. He touched her belly! He was up to something terrible, and she didn't want to know what. These men were dangerous. What was she thinking? She had Ikali and Tessa to think about. And now this beautiful baby. Terror rushed over her. What had she done? Who would bring a child into this insanity? *Chance was dead.* Basel was locked in the basement. She couldn't even trust him with her cats, much less around the baby. What if he poisoned her sweet little infant? She had to get them out of her house. Screw the ruppie. *Screw Mother.* Completing Mother's work wouldn't bring her back or make her love Jaspierre. It wouldn't fix her broken childhood. It wouldn't give her family. Ruppies were so fucking useless. She wanted her dad, her mom, and Lucas. She needed a real, dependable family.

She was desperate, grasping at straws, trying to fix these terrible mistakes. Her whole life was one giant train wreck. She deserved everything she got. *Chance was dead.* Her stomach tightened again and tears poured out of her eyes. Alone. Alone in this clinical room. Nobody loved Jaspierre. This baby might love her if she didn't screw it up. But she would screw it up; she couldn't help herself.

"Honey, is your husband coming soon?" said the nurse. "It might be nice to have someone with you."

"He's dead," she said. *Lucas is dead. Chance is dead. I lit the match.*

"Oh." The nurse turned around, flustered, and quickly exited the room.

How could she protect this little person? She could not protect herself, even. *Chance had to be dead.* What kind of person was she to be a single mom? Dru was destroying her life; nothing was safe anymore. Danger and death lurked around every corner, and even though she had been trying so hard to build a beautiful, safe, happy family for this baby, all she was ending up with was a nightmare.

The contractions started to slow, five minutes apart, ten minutes apart, twenty minutes apart. The further they spread, the happier Jaspierre was. She could go home, grab her stuff, grab her cats, and get the hell out. It seemed like this was the only real solution she had right now. *I lit the match.* Giving birth to a baby alone was terrifying. *I heard his screams.* The giving birth to a baby alone while three dangerous men lived in her house was deadly. *Chance was dead.* Get the hell out.

* * * * * * * * * * * *

The girl was cold and stiff by the time he was ready to leave the florist. Chance took the bouquet she had made and a card. He spent about thirty minutes thinking up and writing a note to Jaspierre. He searched the chick's purse for keys and hit the jackpot. This girl drove a black Hummer, his kind a car.

He took her credit cards and all the cash he found in the store, then got in her Hummer. He had to adjust the seat back quite a ways because she was a tiny woman. Shame he couldn't let her scream much. *That was always so fun.* He drove down to Jaspierre's office, keeping his eyes peeled in case he saw her car. He didn't see her. He pulled his hat down low and turned his collar up, trying to make his scars, burns, and tattoos more subtle. The Hummer thankfully had a pair of sunglasses sitting inside. He slipped these on to complete the look.

He felt a tiny bit nervous slipping into the glass doors. "Can you give these to Jaspierre?" He held out the flowers and the tiffany box to the secretary.

"You know, she might prefer to get her flowers at the hospital. She just left. Looks like that baby is coming today!" The bubbly little secretary barely looked at him, already nose deep in the flowers. He snatched them back.

"Okay." And he quickly left, holding the flowers up to his face to help obscure it from the inevitable cameras.

He drove to a payphone down the street and called the hospital. "Is Jaspierre Kyller still there? Has she been discharged?"

"Alright, let me check. It appears to be that she is still in labor and delivery. Would you like me to ring her room?"

"No, no thanks. I, I just wasn't sure where to send the flowers." He hung up with a swift click. Now he just had to decide where to wait and watch for her. How should he deliver the flowers? Would it be best to wait down the road? Would it be better to wait in the hospital? Decisions.

He got back in the Hummer and zipped down the road to the cabin. He drove up cautiously; no cop cars. He grabbed all the important stuff – porn, beer, guns, bullets – and stuffed it in the Hummer. Then he drove into the woods and waited to see if they would come. They had the truck. They might know where this cabin was. *Damn shame.* He made that room especially for Jaspierre.

He found a decent spot to wait, and once he saw her leaving the hospital, he drove on ahead and set the Tiffany box and the flowers in front of her gate. *Enjoy, my love.* And then he parked in a subtle spot nearby so he could watch her pick them up.

* * * * * * * * * * * *

Edward found the body of the florist. The security footage showed Chance. He didn't look like any of the pictures they had. But it was him. Fingerprinting didn't lie. Hell, the murder scene practically screamed his name. Serial killer Chance didn't give a shit, killed in broad daylight, thought he was untouchable. He was getting sloppier.

Edward assumed that once they cornered

him, there would be a rain of gunfire. Chance wouldn't go down without a fight. Suicide by cop. Or plain suicide. He'd shoot himself before he would ever get locked up. Even fucked up cops didn't fare well in prison. When Edward got back to the office, he had a stack of paperwork sitting on his desk.

He squished into his chair. Two reports were most pertinent. The truck was a red Ford. The VIN number had been scratched up. But Chance hadn't done a great job. They had collected about half the numbers and were running it through a program to help narrow it down. It was pretty likely that once they knew where the truck was from, they'd find his current hiding place.

The dental records for the man at the lake had come through. He was here on a business trip from a couple of states away. The wife had stated he loved to drink and probably got killed in a bar fight. She didn't seem to have much love left for the man; even the clinical report of her statement screeched her anger. He had a picture of the man; he was fat and bald. His name was Tom Dickerson.

Meanwhile, Edward got a ping on Mr. Dickerson's car. It had recently been towed from a nearby bar. He took the picture of Mr. Dickerson and stopped in to talk to the staff. A fit tall bartender recognized the photo. "That's the asshole who was threatening one of the waitresses. I threw him out."

"When was that?"

"Probably around the seventeenth. Let me check the schedule. Yeah, Jen was working on the seventeenth, so that's my guess."

"Do you think he went with anyone? He was murdered shortly after leaving this bar."

"You know, I bet that was his car in the parking lot I had towed a week later. The bar wasn't real busy. Maybe Jen remembers something."

Edward found Jen smoking in the parking lot.

"Yeah, I remember him. He's an asshole. Less men in the country like that guy ain't a bad thing." She puffed a few times. "The chick he left with was driving a nice car. It was black and had one of those... spoilers. You know, a sports car. It looked fast and shiny."

"Do you think it was a Lexus?" Edward's heart pounded with excitement. It was the girl.

"I don't know a Lexus from a Volkswagen. I just know it was expensive and black. That lady comes in now and then, though. She's always wearing a different wig and get-up."

"Do you know how to contact her?"

"She almost always pays in cash, but the bartender might know her contact info." She puffed on the stub end of her cigarette.

Edward wrinkled his nose. Why did the bartender tell him to talk to Jen? He went back inside. The bartender was gone.

CHAPTER

TWENTY-TWO

She lay in her bed, waiting longer and longer until the contractions seemed to stop altogether. The nurse finally showed back up and told her she should go home and only come back if they started getting intense again. Jaspierre gathered her few items and called her driver to bring back her pink Corvette. He offered to drive her home, but she sent him on his way, sliding her belly behind the steering wheel of the sparkling car. She sped home, thinking of Tessa and Ikali and her need to pack and disappear for a bit.

Her mind was focused on the list of things she needed to gather: her duffel bags of cash, her servals, their leashes, and food. Scrap the food; she could just go buy some. Would Dru try to stop her? She wondered if she should wait and sneak out in the middle of the night. But what if the contractions started up again? Better to be in a different town if that was going to happen again.

The pink car whirred up to the gate and it slid open smoothly. She stopped, however, seeing something sitting directly in front of the gate. She got out slowly, glancing back and forth. A slightly wilted, huge bouquet of flowers and a blue Tiffany box sat on the ground. She picked them both up and set them on the passenger seat. Carefully, she looked around. It didn't seem like anyone was nearby. She opened the card:

You + Me and BABY makes 3.

Love, Chance

Oh fucking hell. Chance is fucking alive! She looked around nervously, not bothering to open the box. *Grab the cats and get the fuck out.*

As she drove up her very long driveway, cautiously flicking her eyes left and right, she didn't see him. She didn't see anyone. *Chance was alive.* When she was a child, he was the only one who talked to her, who listened to her, who defended her. Why couldn't she just love him back? Why was it so hard? Why couldn't he be the one? He loved her. In fact, he fucking adored her. He wasn't a nice man, but what were the chances she'd ever be with a nice man? What other kind of true love was there, than when you were willing to kill for each other?

But she just didn't want him. *Chance was fucking alive.* Why hadn't he burned to death? She poured alcohol on top of him before she lit the house. What the hell would she have to do to kill that man? Was she really so incapable? She felt more shaken by his ability to evade death than his ability to completely fucking destroy her. She stopped in front of her house and tried to collect herself.

If Chance could be just a bit different, then maybe he could be family. Maybe he was family; he just offered the kind of twisted love that Mother did. She opened the box to find a finger, still slightly frozen, with a large diamond ring upon it. She didn't feel as shocked as she should have. He was just like Mother, pranking Jasp as a little girl. She almost smiled for a moment. Mother would have fucking loved this proposal. *Chance was alive.*

Her heart was pounding through her chest. *I'll be killed.* She took a deep breath and told the panic to stop. Finally, she decided to grab the box and the flowers and bring them up to her room. *This baby will never see its first birthday.* She would have to burn the finger, of course, not that it was that big of a deal. *Chance is alive.* But she needed to pack her shit, light the fire, and get her cats. And go to Hawaii or something. *This baby won't even make it outside my belly.* Where did people run to?

Chance was motherfucking alive. This was going to mess shit up.

* * * * * * * * * * *

Edward had a message waiting for him on his phone, one of Chance's old teachers. She said, mostly that she wished she could help, but hadn't seen him in years. Edward decided to drive down and see what she knew.

"He was always with that little girl, Jaspierre. Don't you remember? She made the news several times. She's the heiress who had no parents. She ran her company very young."

Edward replied, "I have heard of her. What were they like as children?"

"Oh, she was excellent at her school work. You know, I'm the one who called CPS because her mother wouldn't come in for a meeting. I needed to meet with her, and she wouldn't return my phone calls. I figured it out when I realized Jaspierre had brought in several notes in her own handwriting. She hid it the best she could; that girl was sneaky. Anyway, so I guess they emancipated her, which was nuts because she was so young."

"You said she was friends with Chance?" he said, pulling her back on topic.

"No, I'd say he was friends with her. He pulled her hair a lot. I caught her crying in the bathroom more than once. He didn't like it when she talked with anyone. I tried to encourage her to branch out, make new friends. But he wasn't...

well, he was very controlling. I always hoped that he would grow out of it, but from what you're saying, he's just turned into a monster."

"Do you think she is his accomplice?"

"I don't know. That little girl didn't seem to be violent. She seemed to be tormented, not a tormentor. But people can change."

"Thank you." Edward flew back to his desk with great speed. Chance's old teacher had given them some interesting information. He quickly looked up this heiress. She was beautiful, breathtakingly beautiful. He felt his heart pound unexpectedly quick as he recognized her. She drove the Lexus. She was the one who visited Chance's house! He grinned enthusiastically as he researched her further.

She had been emancipated at eleven, which did seem absurdly young. Her mother been missing since she was seven. She'd been on her own for most of her life. There were great many articles about how she was an incredibly eligible bachelorette. But she didn't seem to go out much; she ran her pharmaceutical company Kyller and Co. and lived a rather quiet life. There was a short piece on how she owned two serval cats, which was similar to owning a lion, as far as he knew.

Why would she be an accomplice? What was in it for her? She was rich, she was famous, she was beautiful and talented. Was she just fucked up? Or was it something else? Did he have something on her?

He felt a little pang of pain. What kind of system was this, where the rich orphans of the world were left to their own devices? Where they had no people who loved them? She grew up alone, completely alone. Her only friend turned into a serial killer. What must that be like? How could she possibly go through that and end up normal?

Time to pay this heiress a visit.

* * * * * * * * * * * *

"Hi, Jasp," Dru said. "How was the hospital?"

"This baby is still in my belly. Not coming out yet," she said. She looked nervous, holding the flowers and the box, trying to slip up to her room.

"I wanted to talk to you about Basel; he seems to have gone missing," Dru said.

"I don't know what to tell you. He's gone. I wish I knew where he went," she said. He watched her carry a blue box and a large bouquet to her room. A short while later, she made an extremely large platter of food and carried it to her library. She locked the door behind her. And about fifteen minutes later, she showed back up with an empty platter. Despite the very early hour, she announced she was going off to bed and locked herself in her room. Dru watched her with great interest.

That pile of food, in that short amount of time, seemed unlikely for five people to eat, much less one. Even if they had a second person in their belly. No, she had to drop that food off, dropped it off for someone. Someone like Basel. Dru slipped into the library and looked around.

It seemed like there must be something. She must've been in there doing something, something sneaky. Dru carefully looked around, but he didn't see anything. She was feeding something, or someone. Dru was willing to bet it was Basel. Now all he had to do was find the poor bastard.

He stared around the room. Nothing suspicious. Books on a bookshelf, a giant marble fireplace with two servals carved on each side. Her desk, large and mahogany, was empty of anything. The floor was long wooden planks and none of them looked like they could be pried up. He stood in the center of the room, slowly surveying, when he finally found a clue. A slightly ashy footprint directly in front of the fireplace. He peered into the fireplace; it looked normal. The ashy remains of a burned corpse still lay in the fireplace.

Russell. If Dru remembered correctly, it was Russell. He stepped back and looked at the outside of the fireplace again. The smooth white marble was cold to his touch. No hidden switches that he could see. He stared at the serval on the left; it was beautiful. He stared at the serval on the right, and the top right ear was slightly smudged. *Bingo*. His fingertips grasped the ear and it clicked.

The fireplace slid away, revealing dungeon-like stairs, down into the darkness. *Well well well, looks like Jaspierre has been holding out on me.* Down the steps he went.

CHAPTER

TWENTY-THREE

Jaspierre rushed upstairs to her room. Once inside, she quickly started packing. She had, years ago, packed about $500,000 in a couple of duffel bags. She grabbed them and set them on her bed, and grabbed two more large duffel bags. In one, she packed lots of clothes, shoes, and all her cat supplies. In the other, she packed blades, wigs, makeup, and any other espionage stuff that she thought she would need. Even a small gun, which she tucked awkwardly in her waistband, although she didn't particularly like them that much.

The total was now four large duffel bags. She wasn't exactly sure how to sneak them to her car, much less sneak them and two large servals to her car. Her fingertips mindlessly spun the little gold ring with the white stone. As soon as she fled, Chance was going to show up. He was such a pain in the ass to plan for. He'd just be mucking around, fucking her shit up.

Flying with servals was virtually impossible. It had to be planned much in advance, to get the special carriers, shots, whatever else it was that they needed. So flying to Hawaii was out of the plan. But driving wasn't safe either. Chance could follow a car; so could anyone. Even with the license plate changer, it wasn't that difficult to note the color of the car or its unusual passengers. Plus, she was going to have a baby and needed a hospital. She didn't actually want to have the thing on the side of the road like some sort of homeless vagrant. It was difficult to decide what to do. If she had friends, she could go hide at their house. But she didn't. If she had family, they could take her in. But she had no family. Tessa and Ikali, as beautiful as they were, could not help her with these kinds of decisions.

She wasn't safe, the baby wasn't safe, and kittens weren't safe. Mother's work would be lost forever, her home left to Dru and his minions. Panic started to set in. She wished she could just fight the bastard, but she couldn't be that reckless with an unborn infant resting in her belly. She felt the strong contraction and doubled over. She tried to take a deep breath. *No. Little baby of mine, this is not the time nor the place.*

She contemplated if she should take the bags to the car or if she should get the cats out first. In the end, she looked over at the finger and blue Tiffany box. Light the fire and burn; that should be step one. Grab the cats, that was step two. Pack the car, step three.

What the fuck would she do if Dru tried to stop her?

* * * * * * * * * * * *

Basel sat in his cell. The cats were silent. The room was quiet. Four perfectly smooth white walls. He knew the door was across from the dark metal rings. The rings sat in pairs up the wall like a playground ladder. They were hell to climb, though, he found.

He could see the observatory glass at the top of the room. Not a single shadow. Just glass.

His fingertips slid across the smooth wall. They froze and his palm pressed tight to the cold wall. A few seconds later, the bathroom opened up. He cupped water in his hands and drank. He was bored as all hell. He'd been in this cell for what felt like a week. She'd bring down a platter now and then, food for a few days. Then she'd vanish. He tried convincing her. Hell, he was fucking mad to be down here. But he couldn't wring her little throat unless he was out, so he had no choice but to wait. He did pushups, and then sat and ate some more of the food. Four sandwiches. He tried to portion it out and not eat too much, but it seemed like he always ran out long before she came back.

He saw a figure in the window. "Hey, so, lady. I get it; I shouldn't have been messing around down here. Let me out now, okay?" The figure waved but didn't say anything. "Let me out now, got it? I ain't gonna do nuthin."

'Cept strangle her. Or punch her in that baby belly, then strangle her. Fuck that bitch. Fuck her house, her money; fuck her up.

The figure in the window was hard to see. Basel stared at it. It seemed like it might not be her. It looked like it might be a man. But before he could determine if it was true, the figure vanished.

CHAPTER

TWENTY-FOUR

Jaspierre walked downstairs, the flowers and the box with the ring-laden finger in her hands. She had every intention of burning it in the fireplace. However, Dru met her at the bottom of the stairs, near the front door. "Well, my fine lady! How nice of you to join us; we're just about to celebrate!" She was on edge, and he seemed suspiciously sweet.

He stepped back and held out his hand, presenting Arnold. In Arnold's arms was a ruppie; no, not a ruppie. *The ruppie.* Her mother's creation was finally complete. The long rabbit ears were perky and straight, the limbs of the rabbit were healthy and alive. The dog was still hooked up to an IV of medications, but it tried to wag its little stump of a tail. Arnold grinned and set the creature up on the entry rug. It scooted, using its front paws to drag a little ways forwards towards Jaspierre. Its tiny back feet gathered underneath it and, with a tiny little hop, it flopped forwards. The ruppie was clumsy but functional. A hopping puppy rabbit! Mother would be so proud. One of her most inventive, creative, exciting ideas had come to life.

It was a second child. Her second child had been born, the first one still waiting in her belly. This was it! Mother was here, in spirit, at least. Jaspierre let out a little squeak. Emotional, hot tears rolled down her face before she could will them to stop. Mother would be proud of her! So, so proud of her. Ikali, Tessa, baby, Jaspierre, and this ruppie. It was family; she had a family. The only thing missing was her father. An emotional sob suddenly burst out her throat. Everything was going to be fine.

She threw her arms around Dru, tears still streaming "It's beautiful!" For a moment, all her troubles vanished. The box with the finger and the ring were still in her hand, completely forgotten.

And instead, she asked, "Is it a boy or girl? What do you think you should name it?"

"It's a boy." Dru's eyes flashed deviously. "It's named Russell."

Jaspierre was in such a delightful mood that she didn't grow angry hearing that awful name. "Well, obviously, he is absolutely going to have a new name. I'm not sure what yet. I think I have to get to know him. Do you think he'll be friendly?"

Dru reached down, petted the long pointy rabbit ears, and the ruppie let out a little bark. It sure seemed friendly; it seemed beautiful in its own little way.

Even her daring escape had been completely forgotten. She forgot Chance, the dangerous Dru, and this baby about to burst from her belly. She forgot all the things she should've remembered.

* * * * * * * * * * * *

Pierre exited the cab, noticing the pink sports car sitting in front of the large, carved marble steps. He stared at the large servals carved into bushes and the glamorous front door. That same front door, all those years ago he stood in front of with Severina. With the woman he thought would be his wife, but instead became his torturer.

Each step seemed long and heavy and terrifying. He had only gone up two steps when the cab squealed away behind him. At that point, he was desperate to turn around and run. But how would that help him? He came all this way, flew that long, tiresome flight.

Another step, and he was certain that death lurked behind that door. Severina would open that door and kill him dead. If he was lucky. Or she'd take him and tie him down and they'd screw, and then he'd live in her closet. For forever. A locked up, fucking sex doll. She would be his every fantasy and terror combined into one. Maybe she'd take him apart again. *Why have I come here?* What was wrong with him?

Two steps left. He stepped up one and felt a little faint. He put his hands on his knees and took a slow breath. Jaspierre could be behind that door. That beautiful little girl who let him out, let him live. The little girl that he left with the monster. *Why did I leave her?*

Last step, then he'd need to knock. This was the worst idea he had ever had in his life. According to the articles he found, Jaspierre had been on her own for many, many years. She was emancipated as little girl. She was alone; he left her alone. He owed her a hello at the very least.

But Severina had no obituary. Where was she? Hopefully, not inside. Not this wretched, torturous house! *But she could be!* She could be anywhere. His heart was pounding harder and harder. His skin trembled, and sweat started to form on his chest beneath his shirt.

It was time to knock. Pierre's bravery faltered, and his knuckles made the weakest, littlest rattle at the door. *Come on; this is for Jaspierre.* He knocked harder, trying to ignore his terrified nerves. The door in front of his fingertips suddenly slid open like butter. Pierre let out a gargled noise of fear as he saw Severina standing there, pregnant. A man Pierre knew all too well was holding her in his arms. A thin gray hair fellow held the door, staring.

Pierre's knees gave out and he fell to the ground.

JASPIERRE'S DESCENT

Chapter

Twenty-Five

Arnold pulled the unconscious man inside. Dru released Jaspierre from the hug. She turned and saw her father. It was unbelievable. It had to be him! Here lay the man she had been searching for. She had a family. Father and this beautiful baby about to show up. Her kitties and her ruppie. Everything was perfect.

"Daddy?" Her voice cracked with happy tears. "How, how did you find me? I have been looking for you."

She rushed to his side and kissed his forehead. Slowly, the man roused. Dru watched the interaction with great curiosity.

"Severina?" he finally gasped, terror dripping from his voice.

"No, it's me, Jaspierre."

"Jaspierre, you look like your mother," Pierre said, fear still lingering. He was still lying on the floor while Jaspierre bent close to him. She reached out a hand to help him up, balancing the flowers and the box awkwardly. "You're wearing the ring I gave her?"

She dropped the flowers and the blue Tiffany box in her excitement. "I knew it had to be from you!" Jaspierre blurted out. The vase rolled across the floor, dribbling water. The finger with the ring on it popped out of the box. Pierre let out a shout.

"What is this? *Have you become her?*" Tears flowed as he scrambled backwards. Fear took over. "Are you taking apart people?" The ruppie hopped closer. "Holy fuck, you made a ruppie. *Or did Severina?*" His eyes grew wide, and his body started to tremble. "*Is she here?*" His voice broke and he scooted, crawling away. Jaspierre stood, confused. The horror on his face hurt her.

"Mother is dead. I was finishing her work. You know she would have wanted me to." Jaspierre's hair rose on her neck. How could he accuse her so? "This finger isn't mine!" she shouted, her anger building. "It's not mine! I didn't do this!" He made it to his feet and turned to run. "Don't let him leave." Dru grinned as Arnold chased the older man. The two of them fell to the ground as he tackled him. Jaspierre let out a furious scream. "I'm not a monster! Stop this, stop it now."

The finger on the floor did remind her of the urgency. Chance was coming. Time to pack the kitties and the ruppie and now her father. She'd have to calm him down later. She felt her belly tighten. All this stress was not good for the baby. "Just hold him; we're gonna go on a little trip together. Calm him down. Don't let him leave. I am gonna grab a few things."

She asked Dru to fetch her minivan. She hustled up the stairs to her room. She had four duffel bags packed and ready. She didn't have anything for a man in there, but there was more than enough cash to take care of them both.

She scrambled down the stairs, lugging the large bags. By the time she was back down the stairs, Arnold had tied and gagged Pierre.

"Stop; he doesn't need all that! Just don't let him leave. He's coming with me."

"Ma'am, if I don't gag him, he'll be screaming."

"Fine, leave it." Flustered, she said, "Put him in the car!" Jasp scrambled to her office and clicked the ear of the serval statue. This was all wrong; everything was going wrong. Pierre wasn't supposed to meet her like this. The fireplace swung open and she floated down the stairs. Basel heard her footsteps and started screaming, "*Let me out!*" over and over in a familiar rhythm. *Let me out. Let me out.* She pressed a few buttons and the cats came running out their glass doors. Quickly, she leashed them. Then she paused. She had to go. *Chance is coming.*

She had to go now!

But.

Could she leave Basel down there to die? She thought of Pierre's face, and how horrified he was. Mother would have no problem leaving a man to waste away locked in a room. But she was better than Mother. *She was in a hurry.* Besides, Pierre would never forgive her if she left another man in these rooms. *She was better than Mother.*

She pressed a few buttons and the door at the top of the spiral staircase opened. In Basel's room, the door slid open. He darted up the spiral staircase, but by the time he was at the top, she was gone.

Dru said, "Alright, I put Russell in the back of the minivan, that little ruppie. I thought you might want him with you. Your bags too."

Both cats leashed, she let them into the minivan. She stood next to Pierre, tied and gagged. Arnold and Dru both watched. Jasp tried to convince Pierre to get in. "We'll talk about it all on the ride. We have to go; it's not safe here."

Pierre silently stood terrified, still gagged and tied, shaking his head frantically.

She tried to pull him into the car when Basel came charging at her. He held a sword in his hand. "You don't lock me up, you bitch!" He charged. She ducked, but his wild swing cut deep into Pierre's throat. Blood gushed as he choked and bled.

Dru's mouth grew tight as he tried to control his desire to laugh hysterically. Arnold stepped forward, mumbling his numbers, but Dru put his hand on his chest. "Let's see what happens," Dru whispered to the gray-haired man. He nodded and they waited.

Basel didn't care who he killed, as long as Jaspierre didn't survive this. "Come on, bitch."

She was more prepared than he was and didn't even fumble as she drew the gun from her waistband. She shot him in the face. He tried to charge her while he bled, but she shot him again and again in the chest. He staggered backwards and fell. She doubled over as a contraction took her breath away. She turned back to Pierre. His mouth was still tied with a rag, his arms still bound behind his back. Her father was dead, his blood still pooling around his slumped body. Her family was dead. Despair choked her thoughts. Why had she let him out? When would she ever learn! Her stomach tightened harder, and she sank down to her father's body.

The baby kicked. She had family left, but not much. She had to save this baby before Chance showed up. Sobs wracked her body as she doubled over with another contraction. Lights flickered in the distance.

Dru and Arnold slipped back inside the house, leaving the dead men and the pregnant woman alone together. Dru said, "Arnold, did you see that there is a prison in the basement?"

She doubled over next to her father and held his cooling body. Contractions came faster and stronger. She sobbed and held him. *The pain was unbearable.*

CHAPTER

TWENTY-SIX

Edward's car squealed to a stop. He leapt out. There was a huge dead black man shot several times lying on the ground. A woman cried out; he drew his weapon. As he rounded the silver minivan, a woman collapsed around a man's body. He was bound and gagged, his throat had been slit, and they were both covered in blood. The woman cried out again and doubled over.

"Ma'am, are you all right?" His gun drawn, he looked around wildly, confused, keeping his back towards her. "Who did this? Where are they?"

He glanced over to her. She looked up with the biggest beautiful sad eyes he had ever seen. His heart beat hard. Her blood-soaked arms reached up for him like a lost little child.

Glancing around quickly, he saw no other assailants. He couldn't help himself; he reached down and lifted her. He almost dropped her and they both stumbled back against the minivan. His body was pressed to hers. Her face was smeared with blood and tears. He reached up and wiped her face gently. She let out a cry and tucked her head into his shoulder. He held her trembling body. "Is anyone else here? Are you still in danger?"

She shook her head. Then she cringed and doubled over. He caught her. "Where are you hurt?" He should call this in. He had no idea what he was walking into; he came to question Jaspierre, not participate in a shootout.

"Did Chance do this?"

She let out a sob. He held her and tried to help her to the car, looking around nervously. Her belly was huge with a baby. She suddenly sat down and let out a cry. She was pushing. "Stop! Don't push!" Her baby was almost here. She looked up with terrified, desperate eyes. He tore off her panties and helped prop up her knees. She leaned forward and, with a soft moaning cry, a tiny head of curly blond hair pressed out. The tiniest nose and eyes and shoulders and her whole body slipped out in a big wave of fluids. He had delivered a baby girl. Unexpected pride welled up within him.

He held the little girl up to her mother. Jaspierre's face lit up as she held the tiny infant. She was sobbing hysterically as she held the slimy baby. "Your daddy is dead. My daddy is dead. It's just us. It's just us. Me and you. We're the last family." Jaspierre sobbed. Edward cringed, listening in on this private moment. How was it Jaspierre always ended up so alone? No mother or father or lover? He tried to think of something to say to console her, but then he remembered. *Shit, the cord needs to be cut.* Edward wasn't sure what else needed to happen. "I gotta call for help." He ran to his car and called for an ambulance and backup.

"Lucille. You are Lucille." She sobbed into the tiny infant's hair. The baby cried loudly with her mother.

A Hummer roared between Edward and Jaspierre. *Fuck.* Edward dropped the radio in shock. A scarred and tattooed Chance stepped out of the Hummer.

JASPIERRE'S DESCENT

CHAPTER

TWENTY-SEVEN

Chance had been watching and waiting for a moment to take Jaspierre. He had been screwing around in her garden, waiting patiently for her to arrive. He had slipped in her gate a bit after she had. "Slipped in" was a bit of an exaggeration since he simply knocked it down with the Hummer. He had every intention of waiting for her to step outside so he could scoop her up. He had a feeling that after she got his note, she'd pack a few bags and be ready for a ride. Accidental sleep had visited him a bit, but gunshots woke him up. *Time to party.* He got out his binoculars; he could see a big black corpse already lying on the ground. A minivan was sitting in the driveway directly in front of the house. He couldn't see anyone else. Jaspierre seemed to be just out of sight, behind the minivan. Waiting seemed to be his best option.

Then that detective drove up with his

lights on. The man walked over to Jaspierre, and he started to walk with her back to the cop car. *Fucking fuck fuckers.* She'd be hard to break out of prison. But the craziest thing happened. She stopped walking to the car and instead had their baby. That damn cop even got to catch. Chance started the car, pissed off, still waiting for his moment. It finally came when that dumbass cop walked away from Jasp while he called it in.

Now or never. His tires squealed as he shot the Hummer right between the cop and his woman. *Who's the fucking knight in shining armor now?* He leapt out of the driver's seat and grabbed the baby. Jaspierre let out a scream. They were still connected by the cord. Chance let out a holler of excitement. "Come on, Jasp, we have to get the fuck out of here!"

He opened the back door and grabbed her while she struggled to her feet. He lifted her in with one arm and threw the baby on her lap with the other. He slammed the door and Edward stood helplessly as they squealed away. The Hummer drove off. Edward grabbed his gun and fired at the tires. He raced to his car and called for more backup.

He followed the black Hummer, desperately trying to catch up.

Jaspierre finished delivering her baby. She had a small knife in her pocket and cut the cord. What the fuck was she supposed to do?

Adrenaline surged within her as she held Lucille tightly. He kept glancing back at her in the rearview mirror.

"Holy crap, that was fantastic. So fucking great! You and me and baby makes three. It's so great to have you back, Jasp. I was thinking we could get married tomorrow when the dust settles. I wanna make a real woman out of you, you know? Now we'll have a real family. I think we should have at least four more kids, up to eight. Wouldn't that be great? I bet he'll have your nose. You've got a great nose. If we're lucky, the girls will have your tits. What's this one? A girl or a boy?"

Jaspierre held her daughter close. "Her name is Lucille."

"Fine, fine; you name the first one. I'll name the rest. Lucille is a great name. I like it."

"Chance, where are we going? That cop is following us."

"I love it when you say 'us.' Hell yes. He's following us. I'll take care of that asshole."

Jaspierre took a deep breath. Her baby smelled amazing, even through all the blood. She closed her eyes and counted to ten. Probably stab him in the neck. That was gonna be how she got out of this alive. He was too busy driving the damn car to fight her right now. "Chance. We're gonna make a great family."

"You're so damn feisty, we sure as hell are

gonna have a great wedding night. If you can keep your hands off me until then."

She wished she had her sword. She had dropped the gun when she held her father. A wave of grief washed over her. *Stop it, Jaspierre. If you want to live, if you want Lucille to live. Then stop it. Fucking stop.* No thinking about anything.

Fucking kill him.

This knife didn't seem long enough to kill. Deep enough to hurt, yeah, but Chance wasn't easy to kill. Although, by the sheer number of burn marks, she was almost successful last time. She had no other choice. Fight or die. Lucille needed her to live.

She drove the knife into Chance's neck. He let out a gurgled cry and turned the wheel. The Hummer slid sideways and squealed to a stop. The cop behind them slammed on his brakes, but it wasn't enough. His car T-boned the Hummer.

CHAPTER

TWENTY-EIGHT

Dazed, Jaspierre awoke on the ground. A loud buzzing sound consumed her thoughts. Her ears were ringing; no, they were buzzing. She kept blinking over and over again. She could see a yellow leaf on a tree, dancing softly in the wind. The arm on her right side refused to move, but pain hadn't hit her yet. The leaf suddenly broke free and spun twice in the air. It started to fall slowly, and a breeze caught it and it jerked back up. Would it ever hit the ground? She felt like that leaf, spinning wildly out of control, never able to touch solid ground. The buzzing was unbearable. Her left fingertips touched her ear, smacking it gently. Would that fucking ringing ever stop? The leaf swirled again and landed next to her, on the left side of her crumpled body still lying on the ground. Slowly, she turned her head to the left. Sparkling red and blue lights were spinning. The cop car was on its side. Inside, the detective was doing something. Moving around, shouting something. She couldn't hear him with all the screaming.

Yes, it wasn't buzzing, it was screaming. She could hear screaming. Her left hand touched her ear again, futilely wishing for the sounds to stop. *She was screaming.* The pain crawled through her limbs slowly and, finally, she knew she was screaming. She could feel her chest heave, her lungs fill with painful air, and her mouth peel open as she screamed again. The Hummer was upside down in front of her. She had been thrown from it. Her teeth clenched tightly together as she tried to hold back another scream that was trying to bubble out her throat.

Her legs writhed against the ground. Her teeth were clenched painfully tight as she rolled her body to the left, staring at the cop car. He was climbing out of the car, shifting his body up through the driver's side window. She pressed her teeth tighter together, willing herself to stop. He had blood dripping down his forehead across his nose and plinking off the end. For a moment, she thought she could hear the plinking little drops of blood falling off his nose and onto the ground. He pulled out his gun. Her eyes grew big with fear. Stumbling, he walked towards her. He frantically looked around, pointing his gun back and forth. What was he looking for?

What happened? It looked like she had been

in a car wreck, but her brain refused to tell her more. He helped her stagger to her feet. "Where is he?" he barked, frantically looking around, lifting her up. "You aren't safe here." Blood gushed from between her legs. *From between her legs.* A wave of panic rushed over her. Her baby had gushed from between her legs just an hour ago. Where was Lucille? Terror completely took over and she tried to run. Frantically, she tried to run and find her.

She staggered back and forth screaming, "Lucille! Lucille! Lucille!"

She stumbled forwards, scanning for her infant, listening for her tiny cry. But she heard nothing. Then her legs betrayed her and she stumbled and fell.

JASPIERRE'S DESCENT

CHAPTER

TWENTY-NINE

Edward carried two cups of coffee. He was exhausted, bruised, and battered. He stepped into the interrogation room to see her. She sat. No wig, no heels; a scared little woman. Her hair was short and brown with silver on the sides. She was, somehow, still stunning. It had been exactly forty-eight hours since the accident.

"Jaspierre, I brought you coffee."

"Where is my baby?" Her voice was hoarse from crying. She took the cup. Her eyes were red and swollen. She had spent both nights sedated in the hospital, chained to her bed.

"We are gonna find her." He begged his voice not to betray him. *Would they find Lucille?* "You've got to testify against Chance. We can let you out of here if you tell us he made you do all this stuff. Look, you shot Basel, unloaded the clip in him. You had gun residue on your hands. They want to prosecute you for Pierre's murder too.

You don't have any witnesses. I can't get you out of here."

Jaspierre's chains rattled as she moved her hand, lifting the cup to her lips. "You were there. You should have saved her." Her left hand scratched at her arm as she drank. Claw marks were evident on her skin. "Let me out and I will find him. I will kill him. Let me out. Let me find her." She couldn't look into his eyes; her body rocked back and forth while she scratched her skin. Both hands were trembling. He would have thought she was an addict. Her left hand tore a chunk of hair out. But she had no drugs in her system. Her coffee cup slammed back on the table, spilling. "You let me find my girl." Her eyes connected with his, suddenly stopping his heart. She wasn't an addict. She was going mad.

His heart skipped. She was right; he had failed her. Here he sat with a cup of coffee. *Drink this crappy coffee instead of holding your brand new baby. This fucking cup of coffee.* His hand ran across his face as he tried to wipe the exhaustion away. Chance had the baby, as far as they knew. The trail had gone cold. He was hiding. Last week, he murdered over and over. This week, radio silence. The man was hiding or in another state. Or dead. There were no leads. Not even a stolen car near the crime scene.

The Hummer was in the impound lot sitting next to Edward's ruined cop car. Did he walk somewhere? After the car crash, it seemed unlikely he could have walked. The man had to be injured. Jaspierre said she had knifed the bastard before the crash. The baby was missing. Chance was missing. Not a single phone call reporting a suspicious man covered in terrifying burn scars and tattoos with a day-old infant.

He stared across at her. She was sipping her cup again, staring off into space, one hand clawing away at her once beautiful skin. Edward had destroyed this woman. If he hadn't left her after he caught her baby. If he had carried them to the car before he called it in. If he had stayed conscious during the crash. *Look at her! She's gone mad.* How could she stay sane? Her father slaughtered, her baby stolen. She set the cup back down with trembling hands, clawing again.

He reached over and took her hands. "Hey." Her intense eyes connected with his, stealing his breath. "I am gonna find her," his firm voice reassured.

She leaned in close, her eyes burning into his. "Let me out so I can kill him."

They froze. Hearts beating, eyes burning into each other's souls. She seemed so powerful, even broken as she was. "What else do you know about him? Where did he go? Tell me so I can get her for you! Testify against him. That's all this is gonna take."

Jaspierre's haunted eyes looked away, then

frantically snapped back. *"Let me out!"* Her whole body shuddered.

* * * * * * * * * * * *

Peter stood in the trees. He was hopelessly lost. All the trees were the same; he had been wandering for days. If he could find a road, he could follow it somewhere. But he hadn't found a road yet.

Roads went places.

His hair had been shaved off. He kept thinking that his mom wouldn't like it. She'd be so mad it was gone. He used to have these long, shaggy curls. When school started this year, he asked her if he could chop them off, if he could have a buzz cut like the other boys.

But she said no. She said it was a rare thing for boys to have beautiful curls and insisted he keep them.

Well, he got his buzz cut now. Jack told him it would be fun, but instead, he just felt... unhappy.

He didn't want his mom mad.

He saw a little flicker, like a bright light whizzing past.

Climbing over a fallen tree, he walked towards the sparkle. He was eight years old, in the middle of second grade. He liked second grade; it was pretty fun to go to school and see his friends. He stumbled on a branch and his knee hit the ground hard. Tiny drops of blood ran down his leg and he burst into tears. He wanted his mom, even if she was mad about his hair. He could grow more curls, probably. He missed his school, he didn't like being lost, and he was hungry. Really hungry.

A little flicker of light danced past him again.

He stopped sniffling and walked forwards. It was a road! The sun reflecting off the cars shone brightly. A car was driving up. He raised his hands and waved them back and forth. The car slowed down, and the driver rolled down the window.

Peter hesitated, but he didn't see any other cars. This might be his only chance, *his last chance,* to get help.

"My name is Peter Mirabella. I am lost and I need my mom. Can you help me find her?"

The man with the thick sunglasses and big hat stared at him. "Did you say Peter Mirabella? I saw your name on a sign." A tiny cry from the backseat tittered through the air. "You can sit by Lucille; shake her rattle if she starts to cry."

Peter got in the back seat nervously. A tiny baby girl with blond curls sat in a car seat in the middle seat.

"What's your name, sir?"

"You can call me Chance."

EPILOGUE

Jaspierre stepped out of the large metal door. Edward smiled at her, holding two cups of coffee. "What's it feel like to be a free woman?"

"Pretty damn nice." She smiled back at him.

"Can I give you a ride?" He ran his fingers through his hair and tried not to stare at her. She was wearing a snug dress, and her muscular, thin body was easy on the eyes.

"Sure, you can drop me off at the office, I guess. I have plenty to do there." She climbed into his car. He had washed it and had it detailed the day before. It still smelled of lemon cleaner.

They rode together pleasantly, not saying much, but she had a grin plastered on her face. "I'm glad you are finally out." He wanted to apologize, but how could he? *I'm sorry your baby is still missing, I'm sorry you have been in prison for four years. I'm sorry?* Guilt curled around him, but that wasn't all he felt. He glanced over at the beautiful, strong woman sitting next to him. She seemed ageless somehow. These long four years had been spent perfecting herself; her body was stronger, quicker, and ready for...

Probably ready to find her baby. He tried not to imagine that she would launch herself into her own investigation, but it seemed like she would be hot on Chance's tail as soon as he dropped her off. He wished she had just given him more information so he could have helped her.

He pulled up to the front doors of her pharmaceutical company. "Hey, Jaspierre?"

"Yes?"

"Be careful." He reached out and touched her hand. She flushed red and stared into his eyes; no, into his soul with that piercing look. She leaned towards him suddenly and kissed him. His heart pounded and he grew red with excitement. He tried to say something once her lips left his, but she placed a finger on his mouth. She leaned in once more and whispered, "*I am gonna find her.*"

JASPIERRE
JASPIERRE'S DESCENT
JASPIERRE'S LAST CHANCE

LANDLOCKED LIGHTHOUSE

WWW.MIXIJAPPLEBOTTOM.COM